REC~~

Praise for *The El*

"While exploring the need for self-e~~
to achieving it, *The Elegant Out* offers ~~
between a second pregnancy and the w~~ ~~ ode to creativity that combines psychological insight with the passionate
pursuit of inspiration. Moving, absorbing, and honestly written."

—JESSICA LEVINE, author of *Nothing Forgotten*

"I lost myself in this story . . . the plot unravels beautifully."

—KRISTEN MOELLER, author of *What Are You Waiting For*

"Beautifully told, this story of a woman at her fertility crossroads
will resonate with many readers. Choosing between the long-term
commitment of having a child and the joyous fulfillment of writing
a novel feels like a downside of being a liberated woman, but working out the answer can lead to insights that expand the heart."

—JENNI OGDEN, author of *A Drop in the Ocean*

"The author convincingly weaves the conflict of a thirty-six-
year-old caught between the biological imperative and the desire
to birth herself as a writer. She paints a heartfelt picture of a
woman in the throws of urgency. Bartasius explores the yearn-
ings for forgiveness toward self and others in this portrayal of
Elizabeth who can't seem to "take those hands off her throat"
and emerge from her strangle hold. *The Elegant Out* offers much
wisdom, inspiration, self-reflection and love."

—BARBARA SAPIENZA, author of *Anchor Out*

"The eloquence of the writing is palpable. Her words paint pictures. More than that, *The Elegant Out* is a reminder we all have
our hands around our own throats choking off our self-expression,
and we all have the power to remove them, should we choose too.
A beautifully written book by a brilliant writer."

—JENNIFER COKEN, author of *When I Die,
Take My Panties* and *Embrace the Ridiculousness*

"From the first line to the last page, Elizabeth is both audacious and subtle in her story and her writing style."

—JOSEPH NUCCI, author of *Bubble Dynamics*

"The novel of the year that you WILL NOT be able to put down . . . Elizabeth's witty, compelling, and fragile voice moved me to the core in a way that left me reading the last words of this novel with regret that they didn't last longer, and feeling ravenously desirous of more of this talented author's stories."

—ABIGAIL SKEANS, ESQ, cofounder of Pomona Society

"Elizabeth Bartasius's wit will have you laughing out loud. Her gritty, steadfast prose offer comfort and understanding. Her heroine's honest tone assures readers that they too do not have to apologize for unflattering, vulnerable, and painful missteps."

—JILL MURPHY LONG, filmmaker and author of three books in the Permission To series

"I love the way Elizabeth Bartasius writes. Abuse is a triggering topic, but she delivers the story with such grace. I felt myself cheering the character on."

—SHELLY BELL, Entrepreneur of the Year, Technical.ly DC

"Stunning prose . . . What a rich and beautiful way to spend an afternoon."

—SHOSHANNA FRENCH, founder of Simple Spirit

"Deep insights, enjoyable characters, a delightful unfolding of an intimate conversation."

—ANNIE ROSE STATHES, social justice performance artist at Be Authentic

"*The Elegant Out* is a true treasure—a story you will turn to time and again for inspiration, heart, and a good chuckle when you need it."

—MONICA MEHTA, author of *The Entrepreneurial Instinct*

THE
Elegant
Out

THE Elegant Out

— a novel —

Elizabeth Bartasius

swp

She Writes Press, a BookSparks imprint
A Division of SparkPointStudio, LLC.

Published 2019
Printed in the United States of America

ISBN: 978-1-63152-563-6
ISBN: 978-1-63152-564-3
Library of Congress Control Number: 2018956763

For information, address:
She Writes Press
1569 Solano Ave #546
Berkeley, CA 94707

She Writes Press is a division of SparkPoint Studio, LLC.

All company and/or product names may be trade names, logos, trademarks, and/or registered trademarks and are the property of their respective owners.

Cover design by Mimi Bark
Interior design and typeset by Katherine Lloyd, The DESK

THIS IS A WORK OF FICTION. NAMES, CHARACTERS, PLACES, AND INCIDENTS EITHER ARE THE PRODUCT OF THE AUTHOR'S IMAGINATION OR ARE USED FICTITIOUSLY. ANY RESEMBLANCE TO ACTUAL PERSONS, LIVING OR DEAD, IS ENTIRELY COINCIDENTAL.

For Corinne,
who has never left

"Resistance's goal is not to wound or disable. Resistance aims to kill. Its target is the epicenter of our being; our genius, our soul, the unique and priceless gift we were put on earth to give and that no one else has but us. Resistance means business. When we fight it, we are in the war to the death."

—Steven Pressfield, *The War of Art*

Hands

I remember the night my son's father put his hands around my neck, choking me, my body pinned to the ground. I hated him in that moment. I thought he would really kill me, twenty feet from our two-year-old son playing in his crib.

I kicked, cried out, and kicked again. It had all happened so fast: his temper, my anger, the hole in the wall, me on the ground, and his knee in my ribs.

Little Jack bobbed up and down in his crib while his parents struggled on the floor, maybe for the last time. Maybe the daddy wouldn't stop squeezing. Maybe he would drain it all out of me. Maybe I wanted him to; I'd lived too long in the little house, in the little town, without my voice, as the man-child I'd married whispered over and over again the only mantra he knew: "Take some Prozac."

Yet, something in me knew he couldn't kill, he

wouldn't. The summer evening was too perfectly warm, and our son too perfectly delightful, happy with slobber dribbling from the corners of his mouth. Like every other project left undone, Tom didn't have the stamina or the courage to follow through.

Tom was only thirty-two. I was twenty-eight. We had our whole lives ahead of us. But neither of us knew at that moment how the hell to deal with the lives we had behind us. I was married and miserable. And he was married and happy, if only I would take that damned Prozac.

I'm sure I called him stupid or insensitive. Maybe I even told him I hated him. I don't remember what I said exactly, only how I felt.

Lost.

Full of rage.

Like at any moment my body would all at once turn leathery and wrinkled, and fill itself with tumors from toes to lips, all from the massive channel of negative energy that I just couldn't seem to purge, no matter how many pages I wrote in my journal.

My neighbor at the time, a therapist living slightly above the poverty line, had asked me if I was sure I wanted a divorce. "You make beautiful babies," she said. "Besides, most women who get divorced struggle financially." She's the only therapist I'd known up to that point, and I didn't have health insurance, so I didn't know "Go to Hell" was the proper response to her loony advice.

Then, of course, there were the wedding photos.

Tom and I had the most beautiful album. It was quite something out of a fairy tale. I loved my wedding dress. I loved the dude ranch with the long, lazy front porch looking over Steamboat Lake. I loved the field of yellow wildflowers that had bloomed exactly on that weekend, I'm sure just for my wedding day.

I was afraid to leave; maybe divorce wasn't such a good idea.

Tom never asked what was wrong or how he could evolve. He just punched a hole in the wall, yelled at me, threatened to take my son away from me, and called my parents to see if they could do anything to set me straight. Occasionally he'd remind me how good I had it; after all, some people have husbands who beat them regularly, he'd say. The bar was set lower, and then lower once again when he put his hands on my neck.

So many days during that four-year marriage, I hoped I would come home and find him tangled up in some woman so I'd have a good excuse to throw a wild fit and call my lawyer. When that didn't happen, I did everything I could imagine to get him to hate me so he would *please* just leave me alone. After one fight, he mock ran out on us. He kissed Jack goodbye, got in his old beat-up truck named Rusty, and drove away. I felt so relieved, so thankful. Thirty minutes later he returned home.

So I had a weekend affair with a man who immediately ordered a cheeseburger afterwards. When room service showed up, I lay shaking, praying that this misadventure would somehow set me free.

But everywhere I went, there I was. I couldn't escape

me. And none of my antics worked. He wanted to keep going, fighting all the time, whether I cheated or not. My father, who only saw the goofy front that Tom wanted him to see, told me I ought to be "thankful for being so loved." Only I didn't feel love present. Not from him, not from me.

On that night, when I finally kicked free of Tom's hands, I ran to Jack's crib side and laughed. The kind of laugh you give when you've used up all the other forms of expression. The kind of laugh you give when you're tired and worn and ripped to shreds like a hash-browned potato. The kind of laugh that comes from somewhere deep inside and makes a sound so guttural, so haunting, that even you don't recognize it as your own laugh.

I relished this foreign, maniacal noise that etched its way up my sore throat and made my eyes burn as it forced its way out of me and onto Tom. That laugh was freedom. For he had shown his true colors; I no longer had anything to lose.

He'd never laid his hands on me before that night, but once was all it took. His hands lingered like ghosts around my neck through the divorce, through a custody battle, through the reconstruction of our separate lives. As the years went by, I fell in love with another and the handprints faded; I then realized I had everything to lose.

Chapter 1

IUD

I awaited the tenth birthday of my IUD with only one word on my mind: expired. Past its ten-year useful life. Copper shine dulled by a decade of dark and damp vaginal fluid. No longer a protector against unplanned fertility, unwanted surprise.

When the IUD went in, my lower half was numb from an epidural and the shock that I was now a mother. Jack, the bright sundial I gave birth to, seemed like an obvious eternal attachment, a little rascal by my side. He would never leave; he would always need me. Unlike the intrauterine device, he would never expire.

Then, even ten years seemed like forever, an always one-day-some-day event, nothing to worry about. Ten years was way more time than I thought I would need to conceive a second child. But during a divorce that took four years, a Hurricane Katrina recovery that took five, and the ongoing potting, planting, fertilizing, debugging, and growing of new love, that IUD hung, nestled inside, growing in age with its twin, my son.

When the deadline drew near, I often wondered if the IUD would go bad gradually or suddenly from one day to the next. If on some Friday night, after a dinner out, my life journey mate, Gabriel, and I would arrive at the nine-year-three-hundred-sixty-forth-day mark, celebrating our last birth control Mardi Gras. What a night! We'd order the 1990 Gaja Barolo Sperss, savor the duck pâté, and gorge on the chocolate pot de crème. Then we'd head home to lit candles, curtains blowing, and sex, unsheathed, as much as we wanted, with no regard for fertility.

I imagined on the following Saturday morning, when the clock struck twelve, if that IUD wasn't upgraded immediately with the new, more modern version, all bets were off. Floodgates open. Eggs vulnerable.

As Jack grew taller and Gabe's roots entangled in mine, I began to think vulnerable eggs weren't half bad. Maybe I wouldn't mind so much. Having another baby. I wondered what it might be like to raise a human wonder with a true partner, a man I want to share bath towels with 'til death do us part. A man who doesn't roll over and say, "You're the one with the breasts, you feed him," but instead, naturally and with initiative, cradles the crying wee babe and grabs a bottle of mother's pumped milk from the fridge, so she can catch up on much-needed sleep. This is what Gabriel would do with a tart newborn blueberry, just as he took Jack, another man's son, under his soft wing. Gabriel took the role of caregiver seriously, treating Jack as his own, taking the squirt on train rides because trains were so cool, waiting in the car pool with all the other Southern mammas day after day, interrupting the bachelor's life of extreme skiing and adventure trips to help pay for clothes-school-supplies-whims-food-travel-medical expenses when Dad wouldn't/couldn't.

Gabriel would make a great father, I knew. He'd proven himself. However, three years before we sealed the deal to spend our lives together through talk of family cell plans and where to store the toothpaste, my love disclosed he wasn't looking to sign a marriage certificate or have babies. At the time, I wasn't either.

We agreed to take it slow and to explore the potential of, as Gabe called it in German, *Lebensgefaehrte*, which he translates to *life journeyman*. A powerful, committed partnership (a tall order by any standards) would do us just fine, and the existing toddler from my expired first marriage was the only child we wanted to smother with our love and attention. Children take a lot of selfless care, after all, and while we would happily give Jack everything, we also had desires of our own. We wanted to live in different countries, walk the Great Wall of China, learn to scuba dive, run an organic farm, or simply have space and time to read a good book in the middle of the afternoon.

What started as a month-to-month relationship turned into a refurbished home in Old Town with cabinets full of knickknacks picked up during Sunday afternoon strolls through antique shops. When I tallied years of arguments resolved, differences navigated, and hurdles leapt, I garnered faith that Gabe and I might actually stick it out. I didn't know for sure if it was the metaphorical bookshelf of "I did that" trophies, or just the biology of woman, but the horizon of tenth birthdays had me thinking of babies. Maybe Gabe and I didn't have to choose between Thailand and a room with a rocking chair. Maybe, somehow, I could still muster the energy to become the writer I so desperately wanted to be, while putting my time in at the office and nutrients into my son's every minute of breath. Maybe even Jack wasn't best served by being our sole focus; maybe he didn't require every ounce of attention, latest-Webkinz, food-made-his-way. Maybe a farting-crying-cooing darling was just the gift we needed on Carroll Avenue.

If it were up to me, I would have haphazardly gotten pregnant and figured out what to do next, but Gabe liked to thoroughly think things through when making decisions. Sometimes, though, he'd shove the thinking aside. Like the philodendron we bought at Home Depot one Saturday afternoon that became root-bound for a year until we finally called a gardener to just plant the damn thing, I knew if I put in a shiny new IUD, the likelihood of taking it out sometime in the next ten years to have another child was probably zero. There are so many other things to tend to when the biological clock is ticking: the garden needs watering, the PTA won't run itself, the homeless need written grant applications to help them get back on their feet, and my grandmother awaits my calls. Another ten years could pass and a third

IUD could be required. Or menopause could take over. Or I could take to smoking cigars and trading options, losing my appetite for diapers.

Besides, the thought of being an older mom didn't necessarily spark my beating heart. Who wants to go through sleep deprivation at forty-six, toddlers at fifty, teenagers at sixty, and eventually grandkids in the seventies and eighties? If my grandmother was anything to go by, that's when I'd want the earned quiet to kick back with a book, plan lunch while I'm eating breakfast, visit the hairdresser every two weeks, and live in a house on a hill where I can say, "I like to look down on people."

Perfectly healthy at thirty-six, I was in love this time—in an authentic adult relationship—and had the benefit of motherly wisdom. My parenting résumé glowed with accolades and hard-knocks experience; I had, after all, been raising a child for the last ten years. I was good to go. If ever there were a time to have babies, it was when the IUD expired and I was thirty-something still.

Before biology said no. Before Jack turned rogue teenager. Before the mood passed.

Maybe Gabe would change his mind.

Maybe I could help him change his mind.

Chapter 2

Haiku

"Hard boiled, scrambled, or fried?" Gabe asked, raised volume, with the skillet in his hand and a kitchen towel draped over his left shoulder.

"Hard!" Jack shouted from the bathroom where he'd supposedly gone to brush his teeth.

I stepped into the kitchen, dressed for work, and stuffed a laptop into my shoulder bag. A sunbeam inched across the brick floor as if ready to pounce on my feet like a cat on scrambling lizards.

"Did you make tea?"

"Over there." Gabe pointed to the single cup with the tea bag string flopping over the side.

"Thanks." I picked up the mug, thinking of out-come measurements. It wasn't even seven thirty in the morning; my stomach swirled with the anxiety of grant deadlines. Dear God, please let the boss be in a good mood today. Sometimes walking into the office felt like walking into my high school history class; I so badly wanted Mr. Peacia to know I was smart and upgrade my B+. I needed to get all A's so I could attend the honors brunch and Mom and Dad would be proud. I wanted my boss to be proud. I wanted to a do a good job. I wanted a goddamn skyscraping thank you of approval.

Gabriel placed the eggs in a pot of boiling water and set the timer to five minutes, then walked over to me, wrapped his arms around me tight, forcing me to stop my mindless shuffling about.

"Good morning, sweetheart." He kissed me on the forehead, dropped his lips to my neck, then worked his way back up the line of my jaw. He stopped to hover in front of my mouth, teasing me with the air of a kiss. My neck leaned forward, wanting more, wanting to cross the breath between us until I landed safely on his side. *God, I loved this man, so doting and sexy.*

Jack came out just then, a long crease in his white shirt and navy slacks that rode too high on his ankles because, like me, they couldn't keep up with the changes taking place in this once-small boy. He thudded into a chair at the dining table, sitting half on and half off.

Gabriel rounded the table to kiss Jack on the top of his head. "Good morning, little sweetheart."

"It's not a good morning."

"Why is that?"

"I have to go to school."

Like every Monday-Tuesday-Wednesday-Thursday-Friday, I went about the to-and-fro routine of getting ready for the day, speed-walking from bedroom to kitchen and kitchen to bedroom, picking out which earrings to wear and packing Jack's lunch bag with applesauce, a turkey sandwich, and a napkin on which I'd scribble a love note or a riddle.

Gabe went about the routine of serving the eggs.

Jack went about eating the eggs. He poked a hole in the white shell and yellow yolk gushed out the sides.

"Gabe, what is your definition of hard-boiled?" he asked, more curious than angry, more inquisitive than irritated.

"Sorry, baby. I can cook it longer next time."

"It's okay."

Gabe delivered my plate and his, and we sat down side by side, a solid team; together we could handle whatever came next.

"I dreamt last night we went through storage boxes looking for a VHR," Jack said without looking up from the egg.

"What's a VHR?" I asked gobbling my food like if I didn't get to it first someone else might eat it for me, a throwback to the days when I competed with a little brother for the Oreos.

"You know, it's that thing that plays movies that aren't on DVD."

"Oh, you mean a VCR?" I laughed, remembering when I was almost ten and my father brought home that most amazing technology. I'd never heard of a VCR, but I was beyond thrilled that I could do something so unbelievable as capture a movie so I could watch it whenever I wanted. *Superman*, which aired on HBO after my bedtime, was the first movie I ever recorded on a VHS tape. VHS tapes seemed a distant memory, barely accessible, as eight-track was for my father. Just another measurement of time, like wrinkles, iPhones, and roach clips.

"Did you brush your teeth?" I asked, trying to remember if we'd forgotten any part of our morning get-out-the-door-for-school-work routine.

"Yes." Jack rolled his eyes and decided he was done talking. He snagged a scrap piece of paper from his school bag. In English class, he'd been studying poetry, so while he ate, he wrote a Haiku:

I don't know, do you?
What day it is, or the time?
Lost in confusion.

No, I didn't know, then.

Time was moving. Fast.

Yes, lost. I felt so lost.

And I didn't understand how a mere nine-year-old could possibly translate my internal state of mind in seventeen syllables at the breakfast table. *God, I loved that boy, so brilliant and unripe.*

"Mom, what time is it?" He finally looked up.

"Shit! We gotta go."

I rushed him off to school, like every morning, behind schedule.

Chapter 3

Thirty-Six

At a spaghetti party, Maureen and I both wore pig-tails. She wasn't normally the partying type, but years ago, during our first year out in the "real world" after graduating from journalism school at CU-Boulder, Maureen had wanted to throw a red-themed shindig.

Our early twenties was a glorious age before elders, bosses, and mortgages told us we couldn't become Hollywood movie directors in five years or less. Or maybe we didn't listen-care-know-better. Either way, Maureen wanted a night with red food, red streamers, red twinkle lights, and red guests. So that's what we did.

It seems just yesterday I showed up to her house, a fresh Go Buffs! alumna in a tank top patterned after a Howdy Doody costume, plaid and the color of a barn. In a picture I saw after the party, I could see that my skinny biceps bulged and were bigger than they'd ever been before. Which was still not very big; not quite the size of a vine-ripe Roma tomato, yet defined and ready for a ketchup fight or a night of salsa.

Maureen wore a shirt in a cranberry shade, I think. There were others there too, other college friends whom I don't remember now, her brother, his friends, her mom, her dad, all in varying hues of brick.

Tom was there too. Those were the early days, before we were married, before Jack took root in my uterus, before a long-winded divorce, when I wanted Tom to be harmless, nice enough, a good choice. Simple-minded and in his mid-twenties, Tom showed up by my side in his usual uniform: stone-washed jeans, a crimson polo shirt, and a goofy grin. He carried a Coors in one hand and a cherry liquor in the other. We liked each other then. And he liked the party, a stage on which to perform, as he ate pasta and wove tales of childhood pranks about swinging a bat over his pleading little brother's body.

"My mom always told me to watch out 'cause one day my brother would be bigger than me. He is now!" Tom said, like he said most things, louder than necessary and laughing like a hyena.

Everyone cracked up; I did too, sipping a screw-top cabernet, relishing the day I'd met Maureen in our broadcast TV class sophomore year. Her hair curled like crazy down below her shoulders, and she had invited me to work on an assignment with her. I had immediately liked her porcelain skin and the fact that she had sought shy-me out; she had wanted me to be her friend.

Two decades ago at Maureen's spaghetti party, dressed in *rojo*, surrounded by radishes and raspberries,

Coca-cola cans and baked ziti, charmed by Tom's bad jokes, I had felt giddy, a sprouting human being. Because of Maureen. I sensed she wasn't just a good choice, but a lifelong choice. We were on a journey together, to make our dreams come true, to write books and screenplays, to have our work read and seen, to beat the odds of mediocrity and sustain ourselves on our creativity. Our friendship had cemented, and together, we two would face whatever came our way.

I couldn't have predicted that I would land in my mid-thirties, unsprouted still, missions of notoriety unaccomplished, dreams of publishing on the back burner.

Four days before my thirty-sixth birthday, months away from a rotten IUD, the duct tape no longer held together the wounds of failure. Thirty-six felt like a new level of failure reached. Thirty-six felt on the verge of being mature, as though I should look like money, act like Grace Kelly, and feel a certain satisfaction in ways that I didn't feel because I still saw myself as the newbie to adulthood who stayed up all night with Maureen in the editing booth procrastinating on our final TV News project.

Sure, my nine-year-old child walked into the kitchen with morning breath every day reminding me that I, indeed, was a mother, a tricenarian, a bona fide big girl, and *not* a college grad. But when I looked at him, I felt (beside the required parental gush of unconditional love) an overwhelming, "Whose child is this? 'Cause I'm too young to have babies."

At nine, though, he wasn't a baby. Neither was I. Yet

I still possessed the same distracting habits I'd developed during my youth: switching projects midstream, binging on Lay's potato chips, sleeping until the last possible moment, rushing out the door, avoiding writing, leaving novels incomplete, wishing-hoping-praying, and engaging in magical thinking without the sit-down-and-get-'er-done to back it up.

I thought I would have published novels by now, like I dreamed when I was sixteen in the back of the Suburban on our family road trips. But novels aren't published on their own, it turns out. My last attempt at writing a novel was a beach read I wrote during snowstorms in Steamboat Springs shortly after I'd divorced Tom. I was such a good girl, disciplined and diligent about waking up at six, heading to the coffee shop, and telling the story of how the Bible Belt unbuckles when Gracie, a stuck-in-a-rut accountant, steps out of her goodie-two-shoes and has the affair of a lifetime. I would type away, getting goose bumps of inspiration as I wrote about how Gracie, her vibrator, and her Southern-style band of Charlie's Angels went whole hog to find that the greatest pleasure is the pleasure you give yourself.

Three hundred twenty-five double-spaced pages and 78,074 words later, with carpal tunnel and hundreds of dollars invested in green tea and blueberry muffins, I finished the sassy, sexy novel, *Conversations with Roberto*. It wasn't long after the word count that I ran out of money and needed to cover the house payment and grocery bill. Like any single, reasonable mom, I got a job writing grants at a nonprofit and stopped storytelling.

Now, with an eye toward the next, non-childbearing decade of IUD, I was suddenly aware that I did not have forever ahead of me. Time wasn't unending like it seemed when Maureen and I met at the park at twenty-two years old to write the next scene of a homegrown short film (which only ever debuted to those two family members who promised not to laugh before it was tucked in a case, forever hidden from the light of day).

"Forever" ceased to exist, just as my mother had warned me it would: "The window of life opens for but a small hour." Four more years of the same old, same old, and I would be blowing out forty candles and singing the same hymns: "I want to be a novelist! I want to have a baby!"

I couldn't bear to hear the scratching of another broken record.

Something, I knew, must change.

I'd better hurry up.

Chapter 4

Echo

The remote control rested on a redwood coffee table, which rested on an Ikea rug with washed-out colors of mustard, sky, tree stump, and bougainvillea. Underneath, a sophisticated hardwood floor propped up a "dorm room" aesthetic, making a $300 Scandinavian sofa appear edgy and cool. Ten-foot ceilings and periwinkle wood siding wrapped the historic Acadian into a pretty bow of a house. Interior designers might have called our décor thrifty and creative. I called it hiding.

Not long ago, before we moved the furniture into our new house, I could stand in the center of the living room and hear my echo bounce off the walls and flow through the dining room into the kitchen. Once we'd lugged all our belongings inside—a floor lamp, the cheapo couch with a matching cheapo love seat and armchair, a gold-framed, thrift-store mirror meant for gowned women in bridal shops, and two red pillows imprinted with tropical leaves, reminding me that I someday want to live on an island—the echo disappeared.

Sometimes, though, I heard another kind of echo, one that didn't come from the canyon of house walls; I heard it like a conscience, guiding me, or sometimes, telling me to get off my high horse. This wise echo was faint, practically inaudible. At first, I couldn't hear it over Gabe's talking, the voices of internet marketing gurus on get-published-quick workshops I ordered online, or the collective chatter of our small Southern town. In our time at the blue house, the internal voice was a faceless, and likely frustrated, muse desperately trying to reach my deaf ears. But one morning, I heard the voice whisper loud and clear, and it echoed through the canyons of my head.

"Get a mentor," it said.

Without thinking, I picked up the phone and dialed an old friend—a writing coach.

"Hey there," she answered. "Have you been writing?" I could always count on Robin to start a conversation in the middle.

"No. Help!" I whined, and then forced a laugh to diffuse the whine, as if that would make me sound less whiney.

"What do you need, girl?"

"I want to be writing again. I'm lost when I'm not writing. It's been too long. I want to be a best-selling author."

"Ha! Who doesn't? Have you ever considered if you are actually willing to do what it takes to be a J.K.

Rowling? To write seven-hundred-page novels? Spend decades of your life writing and writing? Digging deeper into the craft? Are you willing to make it a priority? Are you willing to actually write?"

I didn't answer her. I wasn't sure. Her questions rammed into the gaping insecurity, of "could I?" Was I good enough? Smart enough? Writing a book seemed easy, but writing many, over and over again, sounded hard, not doable, and taking too much time, energy, and resources. I really, really liked sleeping in on Saturdays, for God's sake. And ordering pepperoni pizza while kicking back for family movie nights.

"Look," Robin said, her voice as charged as ever, "you were born to write. Or else you wouldn't be so good at it. You have a passion. But, you don't have to be on the New York Times list to be a published author. You do, however, have to be willing to develop your craft."

"So what do I do? I've started and stopped so many book projects. How do I begin again?"

"Start a blog," she said.

I groaned. "Me and internet technology? Isn't there another way?"

"It's easy. Any idiot can do it. Just write one post a week. You'll find your voice. In a year you'll have a book."

"Okay." I wasn't convinced, but I was desperate for something to stick, so I vowed to follow her advice, hoping this time she would be my savior. We spent another half hour trading stories about Jack and Gabe, her kids, the two pugs, and three men she had dated in one day.

"No keepers, but it was fun," she said. A Northeastern girl at heart, Robin had a Brillo pad laugh that always rubbed me the right way. I felt good in her care, better than I had in a long time. For over a year, I'd been fading into and out of a sadness I couldn't quite tackle. I'd come up for air often, but I'd always dive back down. I'd hoped the renewed feelings of hope and possibility for being published that Robin inspired would hang around.

"Now, go start that blog. Wordpress dot com. It's the weekend, take an hour right now," she demanded. "Send me the link to your post when you're done."

We hung up and I pulled the MacBook onto my lap, reluctant to learn how to set up a blog, but hopeful. I thought of the success of *Julie, Julia*. Certainly, my blog could, would, go that big. Yes, indeed, the magical thinking turned on full throttle, and I felt blinded by the sudden need to validate my writing. Money, readership, bestselling status seemed like the easiest venues to get potential naysayers off my back so I could do and live the way I wanted. I still wasn't able to tap into writing for writing's sake, for the joy of wordsmithery, and the adventure of plot weaving. The act of writing seemed impure then, mixed with agendas, expectations, and shoulds about how much I could write, how often I should write, and what I ought to write. At the time, I thought those restrictions came from the outside. At the time, those pressures slaughtered my joy and left me crippled.

Five minutes into the blog setup, I was bored. I didn't know what to call the blog. I didn't know what to say on the blog. Who would care anyway? And what the hell should I write for an "about author?" I felt the lie in calling myself a writer when I didn't write. The lie added bruises to the collection I already carried on the inside.

Before it could no longer be heard, the echo chimed in once more, "Just start writing. No need for perfection. Just get present to the moment. Write whatever comes to mind in this moment. No one will read it."

"Fine." I gave in, aware of the tightness in my chest.

I opened a Word document as I heard Gabriel fill his coffee cup in the kitchen. He moved forward with everyday life, as did the world, while I sputtered, typing any and everything to see if sparks flew.

What is the meaning of life?

What is my purpose here on earth?

Should I simplify life and move to a remote beach in Costa Rica, or should I dive into the rat race and build a Fortune 500 company?

Should I take cooking lessons? Or a nap?

What should I write?

What should I do?

What should I write?

What should I write?

What should I do?

What I do seems never enough.

Should I burn my to-do list or reorganize it?

Should I go to yoga or clean out the fridge? How long do I have to sit at the computer before I can get up and have a snack?

Staying present in the moment is fucking hard.

My mind drifted into hodgepodges of memory: Jack breaching the birth canal, Tom passed out on the floor until two in the afternoon, Tom's fist punching a hole in the wall, and then his hands on my neck. One night after a fight, Tom had called my parents to tell them of my affair. They rushed over—to my rescue, they said—shouting in the middle of the night alongside Tom. All three of them, a brigade of masters, closed in on me, determining my right and wrongs. They were a frenzy of sharks ready to eat me in the name of love. My parents didn't know they were protecting me from the wrong one. I hadn't had the strength to tell them, or even to see the truth for myself. I'd sunk in a corner, my body convulsing, a cat throwing up a fur ball.

I woke from my memory to hear Gabe unloading the dishwasher. Every clink of a plate agitated me, obstructing inspiration like a metronome of self-doubt. Are you sure you want to do this? *Tink.* Are you sure? *Tink.* Are you sure? *Tink.* Are you sure? *Tink.*

Computer in lap, I dialed Maureen on the cell phone to see what she was up to, to see if she could save me, assure me, help me regroup, distract me, anything—but she didn't answer.

I breathed and curved my fingers over the keyboard again.

"Keep going. You can do it," the echo encouraged.

What do you know? I thought, bitter. My fingers hovered over the keyboard for another minute before they dropped.

"This is important. You can make a difference," the echo repeated my deepest wish.

I can't make a difference when I'm frustrated and tired. I can't worry about making a difference when Jack is still learning about solar systems and sentence structures. I'm needed elsewhere. Aren't I?

"Gabe," I called to him on the other side of the wall, "we need to talk."

I pushed the laptop to the side and left the echo, unheard, picketing, in a drawer, in the coffee table, with the remote control, resting on the Ikea rug in the living room of the blue house.

Chapter 5

Mole

"Let's have a child," I tested, as I walked into the kitchen and grabbed a tea mug from the cabinet.

"We already have a child," Gabe said, taking a sip of his freshly brewed coffee, then wiping down the counter with a wet sponge.

"Well, yes. We do. But biologically, he's not ours. You and I have never made a baby together." The obvious statement even sounded dumb to my ears as I spoke the words.

"Sweetie, I told you when we met I didn't want to have babies."

"That was years ago. You could have changed your mind."

"Why do you want to have another baby?" His question challenged me to poke deeper, to come up with a sound, debate-proof argument. I hated his question (and the hundred times he'd asked it) because it felt like an investigation to which I had no plausible leads. I thought for a moment, maybe two, resting my hand on my chest to steady my anxious heart. Forefinger pressed to my skin, I felt the tiny bump of a Cindy Crawford mole above my right breast. The mole comforted me; it was, and still is, a bodily touchstone, prominently displayed above the upward slope of any V-neck.

I've always thought this mole was special. Quite beautiful, really. Yet, the only ones who have ever taken notice of this mole were curious toddlers, the puppy who likely mistook it for a small piece of hotdog, and my grandmother. Each and every time I've seen her, before the hello hug, she drops her eyes to my chest, places her right pointy-finger on the mole like she is pushing a button and says, "Have you gotten that checked?"

For me, this mole has always been a sign of grace and extra-special-ness, like Audrey Hepburn. I wanted to be admired like Audrey. I wanted to be beautiful like my grandmother. I wanted to be worth-full. Growing up on the tennis courts of Delray Beach, Florida, where it seemed everyone was a rich doctor or lawyer (and therefore valued in my father's eyes) I learned worth-full meant professional success. Dad taught me early on that a B+ was *not* an A. Mom, the wanna-be actress, only ever pointed out the Oscar winners; she had little tolerance for community theater. On the court, only the Wimbledon winners mattered. I wanted to matter. Happy marriages, best-selling authors, self-made millionaires mattered. High achievement was the game; and like on the tennis court, I knew I had to win the match.

Perfection, though, is the weave of a Chinese finger puzzle, trapping the digits in bamboo as the victim resists. Perfection, with all its sophistication and admiration, quickly becomes a paralyzing loop of "not good enough" and net shots—the perfect segue for righteous abandonment. No matter how many honor student breakfasts I had attended, no matter how many tennis matches I won, no matter how many bosses praised my work, no matter what valuable lessons I learned from botched start-ups, no matter how many times Gabe worshipped my newly graying twigs of hair, I never felt like I lived up to the mole on my chest.

I still looked to places outside myself, like the mole, to find validation. Which is exactly why I couldn't have a doctor check the mole for cancer. Nor could I allow Gabe to see I felt scared I wouldn't make it as a writer, scientist, entrepreneur, or professional anything. I certainly couldn't have my own self peering through the microscope to uncover why, behind the rebellious women's lib façade, I secretly hoped I could simply be a mom driving a Gap-dressed tot to tennis camp.

Now, at thirty-six going on IUD-less, I felt desperate for the privilege of a fairytale marriage to a man who would take care of me and leave me well-off like my grandfather did for my grandmother. So that I too could have little more on my mind than sneaking potatoes at breakfast and pointing to my granddaughter's chest, asking her if she'd been to the dermatologist. But I would need a granddaughter first, and my current odds weren't looking good.

"Why don't *you* want a baby?" I deflected Gabe's question with my own—as I would do over and over again in the months to come—and I walked into his arms for comfort as he again told me "no."

"We've already got a child to take care of," he explained, "and I believe there are going to be very limited world resources in our lifetime. I want to make sure we can care for us and Jack. I don't want more responsibility right now."

We both stayed quiet for a few moments, feeling our arms around each other. Eventually, Gabe went back to sipping coffee, and I went about brewing tea, dreading Monday morning and wondering if I too was actually craving less responsibility, not more.

Chapter 6

Die

Mondays were a cliché of back-to-school, staff meetings, and waking up before sunrise to a nasty alarm. Mondays meant forcing Jack to listen to reggae during breakfast in an attempt to prop us—by which I mean me—up with an island fantasy as we headed into another furrow of a week.

I had yet to discover Mondays as the bold opportunity to begin a new project. I had yet to embrace the notion that my job at the nonprofit had catapulted me into being a better writer. At the nonprofit job, I had learned how to organize and use structures to craft narratives. I had learned how to map projects with sticky notes. I built muscle around meeting deadlines by declaring the work "done, not perfect." I achieved success winning hundreds of thousands of dollars in grant awards to serve those in need. Grant writing had helped me build muscles I hadn't yet exercised, or even knew existed. At the time, though, all I felt was stuck in the routine of the horrid J-O-B. Mondays reinforced the rut.

Rather than a tool to fulfill my dream of being a novelist, grant writing seemed to me the fifty-pound weight pinning me to the ground and sucking my creative juices. Resistance became the enemy I battled each day as the desire to write fiction morphed into a pest, amped up on a romance novel binge, which sat on my shoulder and taunted me with story ideas.

Midway through reading/writing/researching laborious statistics about the needs of underserved populations, I wanted to invent a crime of passion or watch two people fall in love.

"Don't give me numbers and data. Tell me about a man standing before you, not your husband, lips like cotton candy. You've tasted them before when you were both young and poor, eating satsumas, hidden in a grove on his family farm. Now he's back, ten years later, after the drought, after your parents wed you off to a respectable man with a pocket watch and Italian leather shoes that left black and blue heel prints on your face. Cotton Candy wants you back. He's never stopped loving you, he says under the hundred-year-old oaks with Spanish moss dangling in silence from the branches like the secrets you've buried inside. Tell me that story!" demanded the devil of a monkey muse.

Grant writing is important, of course. I felt proud to spend my days making sure the homeless got funding for homes, veterans got back on their feet, victims of domestic violence and their families had a safe refuge, and those who lost their homes in Hurricane Katrina once again had a place to hang their hearts. It was all very respectable work. When others heard what I did, they approved. On the contrary, when I told people I wanted to write, they'd look at me like I was one of those nutcase, artist types. Doing useful work and being respected was important to me, maybe more important than writing fiction, as my father had groomed me from a young age to study "something practical at university; not drama, like your mother."

As much as my groomed and coiffed practical side talked sense into my silly brain, that delightful bastard of a monkey wouldn't shut up.

"What the hell happened to joy? Joy, for joy's sake!" The monkey muse had a point. Spreading joy is as much a social service as is mental health counseling or rental assistance. Housing is indeed a basic need that many do not have, but for most of the home-ridden, middle-class, first-worlders, if one cannot find pleasure in her own temple, then the roof overhead is but a place to keep dry as one wilts into death. Over the years, I've learned to fight for happiness, to hold onto it with all I've got, to demand it. Like the protesting echo in the drawer, like the monkey on my shoulder, I glitter up the signs and stand in the picket lines. I flail my arms and shout at the top of my lungs no matter how many times society-mediocrity-naysayers-judgments-perfection-my-own-insecurity insults me, tear gasses me, arrests me, batters me with its police sticks. Again and again, I get out of jail, into the open, where I can breathe and laugh again, create.

Because, sometimes, that's just what it takes to keep living in joy.

On that Monday, though, I felt handcuffed. As I listened to reggae, longing for a different life, driving the track to work, and cranking out another grant proposal, writing nothing of my own creation, I felt the secrets that I'd buried inside me settling deeper into an inescapable catacomb.

"Miss Elizabeth?" the receptionist called over my intercom. "Can you help out with Miss Stacy? She wants an update on her application. Everyone else is at lunch. She's on line one."

Uggg. "Sure." I picked up the phone and greeted the client.

"Hi. Can you help me? I hope you can help me because I keep calling but no one can help me. When is my house going to be ready?" the woman on the other line demanded with a voice scratched from years of smoking.

"Sure, Miss Stacy, let me look up your status."

She didn't wait for the update, instead she rattled on about all those asshole FEMA guys.

"I understand. That must be frustrating," I replied, on a replay loop.

"And I'm sick," she droned on. "You name it, I've got it. Rheumatism and arthritis, asthma. Now the doctor says I have diabetes, chronic fatigue, fibromyalgia, and I'm getting treatments for breast cancer. I may have lung cancer; I'm seeing another doctor on Thursday. I take twenty-five different pills. Pill bottles everywhere. I can't even walk without my walker. I need this house now."

"Shit, she doesn't need a house," said the monkey in my ear. "She needs a coffin."

"I understand, ma'am. This must be frustrating for you. I know it's a long process. I wish it were faster. Your application is in the review stage." It occurred to me that the gritty woman just wanted company rather than an actual update, so I listened as she munched down on my ear with complaints.

When I finally escaped Miss Stacy, I picked up my cell to call Maureen, and as I listened to the ringing on the other end, I imagined what it would be like to have dozens of serious health conditions and end up dead.

I would miss Jack and Gabe. I would miss Maureen.

For sure, I would miss the long auburn curls that twist and cascade down her head like bunches of Hawaiian leis.

And teeth as white as Caribbean clouds.

I would also miss her four-minute phone messages, always from the road, usually including a rant about only getting a couple hours of sleep the night before or the rudeness of customers at checkout lines: "Can't these people read? When it says 'twenty items or less,' it means twenty. Twenty! Not fifty-two. Jeez! What's wrong with people?"

I would miss her incredible sense of integrity, knowing from the depths of her soul what is right and what is wrong.

I would miss calling her back, getting her voice mail, and leaving an even longer ramble. Which is what I did just then.

"Maur-eeeeeen!" I sang it like a melody, then threw out an exaggerated Southern-slanged "How are ya?" in honor of my then-current Mississippi residential status. "Why is it so hard, Maur-eeeeeen? This life? Why so hard? Come rescue me, pleeeeeease?" I tried sounding like I was making fun of myself, but I probably didn't pull it off.

"Work was terrible today. My boss went crazy. This woman called and complained about her twenty illnesses. What am I doing? God, how did I get this way? Auuuugh, I wish we could travel back to those college days when we were full of possibility. I mean, I'm trying. I promise, I am. I'm trying real hard, but some days I just can't take it anymore. And I'm tired of being nice. Maybe I could become a real bitch. Say nasty things to people. I've never done that before."

Her machine cut me off, just like that, and I thought back to a time when Maureen lived down the street. We didn't have to dial a number; we could just pop over for a hot dog at Mustard's Last Stand. In those days, she ate peanut butter crackers, then maybe some yogurt, maybe some granola; take-out trips were a treat. As an adult, she switched to Whole Foods and joined an organic co-op. She married and moved into a planned community, modeled after the Truman Show, in a house thousands of miles away. She was so far away that the only way to pop in with her was to leave voice messages.

Not only did I feel far away from her, I felt far away from myself. On my way home from work that Monday evening, I tried to dig up some memory of who I was at my core. I thought back to middle school, before bills arrived in my name, before any living creature counted on me for food and watering, and before my creativity butted heads with Tom's chokehold and Dad's mantra to be practical. When I was young, I'd head to the back-yard after school and play soap opera, inventing all sorts of plot lines with J.R. & Bobby Ewing. In true *Dallas* style, I imagined myself in ball gowns and Western hats. I declared myself the trusted twin sister to Pam Ewing (because she was my favorite character), instrumental in a plot to bring her and Bobby back together. Yes, even then, as a twelve-year-old with friendship pins clipped to my shoelaces and three Swatch watches wrapped around my wrist, I had stories in my head.

As a middle schooler, I got the stories out through playacting. As an adult, I got them out through writing. Only I wasn't writing and hadn't been for years. With each day, another blank page left behind, Robin's question— "Are you willing to do what it takes?" —closed another padlock.

When I got home, I dropped my bag to the ground as I entered the front door and walked to Gabriel, who sat on the couch in the living room of the blue house reading a copy of *Die Zeit* his mother had sent him.

"Hi, love," he said as he lowered the right corner of his foreign newspaper and poked his cheek out for me to kiss. "How was your day?"

"Groovy," I said, sarcastic and kissing him ten times on each cherub before I landed on his lips. They tasted of coffee and sunscreen.

"No wait. Keep kissing me." He make-believe pouted.

I laughed. "You are pathetic." Then, I kissed him some more. Happy to do it. Thankful he was there to kiss.

"What was your day like?" I plopped back against the couch, taking in a long slow inhale, surprised at how good it felt as air filled my belly and moved up through my lungs.

"I got a call from Albert today."

"Nice. How is he? And what's-her-name?" Gabe's cousin and fiancée lived in Berlin, in an apartment with a sunny balcony, far from our everyday lives.

"Anka."

"Yes, Aaaaannnnkaaaa." I said it again real slow, as if that would burn her name in my memory. But, I knew it wouldn't. Next time Albert called I'd ask for her name again. "So how are Albert and Anka? They pregnant yet?" I'm not really sure why I asked the p-question. Maybe it was because Albert told us a while back they were "trying" for a child. More likely, I wanted to plant another subtle seed for Gabriel to reconsider having a baby with me. The question backfired.

"Yep, they just found out. How did you know?"

"Really?" I went quiet for a moment. Then, for the second time that day, I went on autopilot, "That's great." Because what else do you say when someone calls to celebrate their good news?

Chapter 7

Headache

I remember the night I called the emergency room, fumbling in the dark hotel room, after midnight, for a phone number. Not wanting to wake baby Jack. Not wanting to wake Tom.

"Have you had a migraine before?" the nurse asked when I told her what was happening.

"No, no, never," I told her. I didn't know what to do. I could barely open my eyes. The pain had engulfed me all day at Barnard Square and Forsyth Park and followed me into the Colonial Park Cemetery as I searched for an ancestor's headstone. I didn't want to tell Tom how bad I felt. I didn't want to ruin my one weekend trip to Savannah. I didn't want to appear weak.

The nurse gave me directions to the emergency room. There was nowhere else to go in the middle of the night, and there was no way I could operate a motor vehicle.

I put my hand on Tom's sleeping body. "Please, I'm sorry to wake you," I said. "I can't drive. Please take me to the hospital. I don't know what's wrong, but it hurts so bad. Please."

He mumbled, his breath gross and stinking already. I could smell tequila sweating from his pores. He'd gone to the bar earlier, because he wanted to, and because I wasn't much fun with a headache. Since I had stayed in bed, Tom had decided the baby could stay with me while he went out. I hadn't any will or strength to argue. He'd left Jack, ten months old, in the portable crib next to my incapacitated body.

"Please, please wake up." I shook him a little, afraid. I knew he'd be angry. But I couldn't drive. I couldn't think. God, my head hurt so badly. Was I going to die?

"I have a headache, it hurts. You have to take me to the hospital."

"Take an aspirin," he growled from under his pillow.

This wasn't a normal headache. I didn't know what it was, but I could imagine that at any moment a vessel would rupture and I would be left in that hotel room, blood flowing out of my head, my husband sleeping peacefully 'til late morning when he was ready to wake.

"We've got to go. Get up," I said, slowly getting dressed, as if I could stall the pain by being slow, or quiet, or dark, or forgotten.

"Fuck, Elizabeth!" But he got up. "I'll drive you, but that's it."

While Tom waited, I gathered the baby, the diaper bag, the scribbled directions to the hospital, and my crumbling self.

We got lost on the way. We didn't know where we were going. A wrong turn added another forty minutes. Tom shouted most of that time. "Goddamit! Why the fuck do you need to go the hospital? This is so stupid." He didn't stop until he pulled the Pathfinder up to the emergency room doors, and I fumbled out of the car.

I cringed at the bright white lights of the ER, and felt my way to a nurse. I think I filled out some paperwork, with my eyes squinting and my head a sidewalk beaten by a sledgehammer. A blurry doctor moved me into a room.

"We have to do a cat scan to make sure it's not an aneurism."

"Okay." Anything, anything, just please make the pain to go away.

I sat naked, a needle in my back, then nothing. Whiteness, sleep, no pain, no Tom.

When I opened my eyes again it was some time later. I lay on the table, unaware, drugs still in me. I could only see in shapes and blobs. I remember a Tom-blob walked into the bright, cold room, and threw our son-blob into my arms. I could barely feel my arms, I could barely hold him, my sweet baby, but I knew I had to hold tight. I couldn't drop him on the hospital floor. Hold on. Hold on. Hold on.

The doctor came in then and said something to Tom. She sounded angry; he snatched the baby from me. I closed my eyes again and slept.

In that hazy fog of a night, I became clear that Tom

would pay for how he treated me and our son for the rest of his life.

A month later, when we got the hospital bill he shouted again, "A three-thousand dollar headache? Are you kidding me!?"

A year later, I left him for a weekend to have an affair.

When he forgave me that, I divorced him.

Chapter 8

Selfish

I never wanted to be a mother. Not after spending the younger part of my life babysitting my little brother and cousins, while the grown-ups went out to wine tastings and galas. I vowed I would never have kids of my own. They were too much trouble. I wanted to remain unencumbered, free to do as I pleased.

Three years into the fog of a disintegrating marriage with Tom, I noticed a few pains in my belly. Four weeks passed with no bleeding, and I made a side trip to the pharmacy. I remember sitting on the bathroom floor watching a plastic applicator, dreading the color change, and at the same time feeling hopeful. The hope must have come from those primal maternal instincts of amazement and absolute protection of the unborn creature growing inside; biology could be the only explanation for my excitement in an otherwise somber time.

Truth was, I intuitively knew I was pregnant. I knew

before I missed my period. I knew before pink parallel lines told me so. That's why I had declined a glass of wine at our friend's wedding. And why I would go walking in the woods and put my hand on my tummy and say, "Hello in there." The pink lines simply confirmed what I had already known. But, somehow the geometry gave me permission to fall head-over-heels in love with the little kidney bean-shaped parasite.

Love. I felt such love.

Then, horror. I could not raise this beautiful creature with a man who was so volatile, so childlike himself.

But how would I be able to raise this child on my own? I was too scared to leave the marriage; I didn't know where to go. I had to stay, I told myself. Pretend. I could pretend. For the baby. I could do that for my baby.

Turned out, I wasn't so good at pretending. Every time Tom and I fought, I cringed at what Jack might be interpreting. What would his one-year-old, two-year-old, three-year-old mind think? How could he learn healthy relationship skills from two people who so clearly didn't understand the game themselves? How could he be happy in this madness? How could I? After a few years, it became clear to me I couldn't be that woman who stayed, who gave up her entire self for her child. Eventually, I garnered the wisdom that doing so is too much burden on a human being, let alone a child. Still, I felt like a failure. Tom reminded me over and over that I had destroyed our family. "You are so selfish! You have your head in the clouds," he'd say, lips in a snarl. "Jack needs his mom and dad together."

Even as Tom shot verbal bullets, I reminded myself what I believed Jack needed: a mamma with spunk, life force, and a fierce commitment to exploring the nooks and crannies of her life and its evolution. How else would he learn to explore and honor his own? Of course, sometimes life and its evolution got messy. Real messy. But authenticity was worth every bit of grind, and crappy truth was better than faux pristine.

My mothering term, thus far, had been a dichotomy of loving my job as a parent and praying I could be "on break" to write or travel or take a nap instead of making egg salad. While getting on the floor and building Lego structures had never been my thing, hugs and kisses and cuddling came effortlessly. I was enamored with the brilliant little mind that invented his own board games and wrote hilarious tales about Indiana Jones and the Temple of Cornflakes. Before he turned middle schooler and worried about looking good, he was a sound machine with vocal chords constantly at play, buzzing, beeping, humming, whizzing, whooping; I could listen to him all day.

Sometimes when I got home from work late and Gabe would be buried in his home office, Jack would call out from his room, wanting a little attention, "Mom, can you get me some orange juice, please?" He'd already been home from school for a couple hours; he'd likely finished his homework and edited a new video he'd created for his YouTube account: Chocolate Thunder.

"Sure," I'd call back.

I loved him so much. So fucking much.

Loving him was easy.

The hairy part was figuring out how to not screw him up. How could I grow this child so that he became his highest self? The discipline, the encouragement, knowing when to be firm and when to leave room, are hard. As he grew older and became more resistant, my job as his mother toughened. As he was about to turn ten, and the IUD neared its end, I questioned if I really had the energy to raise another. I'd lost the spunk I promised to model for my son, and I wasn't exactly sure why or how to get my pep back.

"Maybe I'm ill," I complained to a friend one day.

"Are you eating enough protein?" she asked. "Don't worry, you don't have cancer." She rolled her eyes as she read my thoughts.

"That's a relief," I said and laughed.

"Eat more meat," she ordered.

I didn't think it was just the meat. Robin's writing advice megaphoned in my head: "Just write one blog post a week." For lack of solutions, I finally sat down with my laptop and logged into my blank Wordpress site to write a selfish, sloppy blog post, all for myself, with no concern for editing. Like a stalled, rusty, busted-ass train creaking its way into movement after a decade of neglect, I typed my heart out:

After a woman has spent the entire day making sure the policy report is turned in on time, the case review procedures are written clearly, and she restrains herself from accidently throwing the office equipment through a stump grinder. . . .

. . . after she's fed herself ten times a day to keep the blood sugar levels at optimum performance, folded someone else's clothes, made dinner on time so that homework could be completed on time, so that the little one could be in bed on time, so that he could stay focused and happy and ungrumpy the following morning when it starts all over again. . . .

. . . after a woman has made sure that the bacon was cooked not-too-crispy-and-a-bit-chewy, even though she likes it extra crispy . . . after she's ruined her good red shoes in the mud, hanging the Spring Fling sign at her son's school. . . .

. . . after she's let her partner make love to her finally. . . .

. . . after she's returned the last phone call for the day. . . .

. . . after she's wiped someone else's pee off the toilet seat. . . .

. . . well, doesn't she deserve to be a tad bit selfish?

Besides, when a woman (okay, I won't speak for all women), when I have not been selfish, even just a little bit, I start to have the desire to stomp on children's toys, to break dishes, to drive wildly into a white picket fence.

When I have not been selfish, I cry. I rant. I rave. I complain. I bite my nails. I shout out when he asks me for a glass of orange juice. I withhold sex. Worse, I don't even want to have sex.

I stop showering. My armpits get sticky and smell. And life with me is hell.

So really, oh you dear demons from the past, YES! I am selfish. And yes, this blog is all about me. And yes, had I not been selfish, I would have made your lives more miserable that you already think I have.

So, let's all go on a selfish ride. Let's embrace our selfishness.

The Elegant Out

Let's print T-shirts with the message, "I am selfish, watch me do what ever the hell I want."

Starting with this blog. My selfish blog. My dirty rotten scoundrel of a delicious, decadent, selfish blog.

It's great to have a spot on the planet, a tiny little space in and of this world, where I am free to be selfish, whiny, beautiful, grumpy, funny, a rotten mother, mother-of-the-year, flustered, depressed, a slob, antsy, flighty, crying, friends with a vibrator, a dreamer, a story teller.

My own special place where I'm free to create empires or be resigned. A place to do yoga, play tennis, suffer Facebook trauma, eat sushi, have the worstest day of my life, put the toothpaste wherever I want.

My own nook to live in a world of possibility, or settle for less. And finally, thank the Lord, a place where I can lift my head in the clouds as much as I can stand it.

Mine. Mine. Mine. Mine. Mine. Mine!

Guilty as charged.

P.S. I really do hope more than one person reads this.

Chapter 9

Changes

Friendship weaves a narrative, with plot points and climaxes, tension and comic relief. Friendships are a source of love and companionship, support, play. Challenges, heartache, pain. Maureen and I had fought the last time we'd seen each other; we'd hurt feelings, bruised hearts. All normal experiences over decades for long-haul friends.

I sipped my third cup of green leaf jasmine at the Japanese Tea Garden in Golden Gate Park. Gabe and I were in San Francisco for the weekend to attend a wedding, and I was already a bit on edge, trying to pretend watching Gabe's friends say "I do" hadn't brought up a few of my own insecurities regarding Gabe's unwillingness to marry. When I found out that Maureen and her husband, James, happened to be passing through San Fran on a road trip down the California Coast at the same time, we planned a rendezvous. I couldn't wait to see her; I needed my friend.

Like butterflies, Maureen and I flitter toward each other at certain points in time, then retreat in opposite directions, then back again. She'd been there for me, holding my hand through the divorce and riding shotgun when, after Hurricane Katrina, I needed to drive the last surviving contents of my home across country. She'd been there for me always. Yet, I felt uncertain, like maybe she wouldn't show up, or maybe she was still angry, or something was left unsaid and she'd decided to drive back to Colorado. She and James were late, very late. With each minute they didn't arrive, those little anxieties populated like fleas.

The San Francisco day was sunny, though, as it always seemed to be when Maureen was around. The time she came to Michigan to visit me during my first marriage, we had an October Indian summer. After my divorce, in New Orleans, we strolled around the Garden District under a pleasant sun, visiting the famous aboveground St. Louis Cemetery and admiring the mansions on St. Charles Avenue. During a January in Steamboat Springs, we sledded in perfect white powder. We laughed and played, and I didn't remember being cold at all. In San Francisco that day, as Gabe and I sat in the teahouse waiting for Maureen and her hubby to arrive, the weather was perfect yet again. I knew full well how windy and frigid San Francisco could be, so I decided to push away the concerns and take the dazzling warmth as a divine omen.

Thirty minutes later there was still no sign of them. All my worries came front and center, compounding like financial investments I wish I had. What if she hadn't forgiven me? What if Gabe never wanted to marry me? What if I had to leave him in order to have another baby? What if I wasn't cut out to be a writer?

Gabe and I finally paid our bill, a full hour and a half after ordering, and traced our steps back through the meandering gardens of bonsai and water lilies. Slumped, I started to ask Gabe if we could go back to the hotel, when I saw Maureen rushing toward me in a wide-brimmed hat—James just a few steps behind.

"I tried to call you so many times. We slept in. Didn't hear the alarm. I'm so sorry," she said, out of breath, as she hugged me.

"We left our cell phones in the car," I said, irritated that she was late, and irritated that the closest I would come to marriage with Gabe was our family cell plan. But I certainly wasn't prepared to admit either of those sentiments. I reminded myself to just be happy she showed up at all; it had been a year since we'd seen each other.

To ease the awkward reunion, the four of us set about wandering through rows of roses that bloom through the summer in Golden Gate Park. James and Gabriel rambled up ahead, talking, getting to know each other better. They'd only met a few times before, yet they were linked because Maureen and I were linked. Linked in the way friends for a lifetime hook together: sometimes from choice, sometimes from obligation, and at times, from a stubbornness that forced the friendship to prevail, no matter what. Stubborn is where we were that day. We were devoted still, despite having given up screenwriting over a decade ago. Despite the fact that five years of geographical separation, differing desires, and the nameless weather patterns of life had distanced us.

We lingered behind our chosen men, trying to find a few moments alone. We needed those moments; the threads of separateness remained unwoven, unspoken, and we had to find a way of continuing our weave. I stared ahead as I walked, the late arrival already forgotten; I was simply glad that we were finally together.

"I love reading your blog," Maureen said.

"Really?"

"Yes! Damn! You've gotten to be a great writer. Not that you weren't one before, but I can definitely tell you've been honing your skills."

Her praise made me happy. And relieved. Maybe I could be a writer, then?

"I totally think you should send that post about your home and the past foreclosure to *Newsweek* as an article. It's so well written and poignant. So many people are going through the same thing, so it's very timely and current."

"Thank you, maybe I will." I linked my arm in hers, the giddy college feeling returning. "You are the best fan ever! Will you remind me now and again that you like my writing? Maybe even call me out on it when I don't write?"

She laughed. "Yes! And if you don't write, I will tie you down in the snow and make you write."

I grunted; she knows how much I despise being cold. "That would do the trick. What else is going on in your life?" I asked, appreciating how friendships have a way of falling quite easily back into place, despite differences and distance.

"James and I are trying to have a baby."

"What? Oh my god . . . really? I . . . really?" I gaped. "Wow, I can't believe you want to have a baby. I remember you sitting in that house we lived in senior year, homework papers all around you. Remember that dirty house? I hated our roommates. I think they threw a raving party every night. I could never sleep."

"Oh my god, it was like a frat house," she groaned.

"And you told me you never, *never*, wanted to get married and have children. Now look at you!"

"Yes, I know." She said it dreamy-in-love.

"Shit! Wow . . . how long have you been trying?"

"Just a month. Some people said it might take a while.

"Or maybe not." I put my hand on my empty belly and conjured up a memory of what it was like to carry a being inside me; how quickly it had happened.

"Are you sure you want to have a child?" I asked her, as she'd seemed so opposed to motherhood before.

She laughed. "James has promised he would take care of it. Believe me, I'm only going to do this once."

Her words satisfied me, and so did the look on her face, like she'd just eaten the best cheesecake and was now ready for the check.

"Let's have babies together." I linked my arm around hers again, a tad excited that dual babies could be a real possibility.

"Do you want another one?"

"Yeah, I think so." I shrugged the words off like it was no big deal.

"Does Gabe?"

"He says he doesn't."

"So what will you do?"

"Nothing for now, I guess. We'll just have to wait and see." I detested waiting and seeing.

"James and I were talking earlier," she said, "We think Gabe would make a great father."

"Would you tell him that, please?"

"He just *has* to want to have children." She spoke with more desperation than I'd shown.

"I know, I know. I'm thinking he'll come around. If I work on him a bit, he might be persuaded. It would be so fun to be pregnant together. We could paint our bellies and make a memory cast. We could shop for cute little hats and compare morning sickness," I said, noticing that all my motherhood fantasies took place during the nine months of gestation, none in the years after birth.

The warm sun and pregnancy talk made me feel rather good. Maybe we could be fat and happy one day, sitting side by side, snickering and eating chocolate chip cookies like we used to in our college dorm room.

I touched my belly again, thinking of Gabe and the "should we?" conversations we'd been having. Despite glorious weather, I suddenly got chilled. I didn't want to tell Maureen that the question of having a baby was on my mind constantly—that I could feel the weight of that question inside me, growing into a very big deal.

Chapter 10

Blog

Two weeks went by and I hadn't written a thing. Maureen left a message on my voice mail: "When is the next blog post? Your fans need it." My fan club remained in the single digits, including Maureen, a few other girlfriends, and maybe my parents if they ever got online.

Robin said in one of our writing coach calls, "You have to share your posts on Facebook. Tell people. It's just because you don't advertise yourself."

True, I didn't, because I did *not* want to write a blog. Not really. Blogs as I understood them were meant to "market" my writing, but I didn't care about marketing. I just wanted to write. Besides, what nutcase has time to market herself when life is already full with working-mommying-chauffeuring-wifeing-busying? In my thoughts, I could hear those same auto-responder excuses that had been passed down for generations. The never-ending parade of time-money-safety rationalizations marching through the ideology of normal folks on public streets, in the nursery schools, in writing groups, on the internet. While rationale may be their guise, the perpetrator is no less than fear. So great are the artists' jitters, it's no wonder Barnes & Noble stocks a slew of books on how to conquer them.

Yet, I carried on with the assertions of why I couldn't do the work. Those innocent bystanders I called family, friends, neighbors, coworkers, and strangers in the checkout line were the soldiers in the trenches, blasted over-and-over-and-over-and-over again by me defending my limitations. I made such a good case against myself as a writer—the arguments were rarely challenged. Who would bother to dispute the plight of the overworked mother? No matter how many do-gooding souls awarded me an innocent verdict, I would simply craft another story about why I couldn't-wouldn't-shouldn't pursue the gift I'd been given. I don't know if anyone actually believed my alibis of motherly-wifely-altruistic duties. Perhaps they too needed to hide from their deferred dreams, and so granted me a pass. Or maybe they were busy digging their own holes; they couldn't be bothered to help plug up mine. Maybe my women friends too felt pulverized by the terrifying "what ifs" and couldn't see their way out of an all too familiar, gendered-excuse fog. So really, who has time to advertise, or even write, when one is scared to death that they might actually have to test hopes and dreams? To test whether or not she is valuable for more than making babies?

At the same time, I sought vindication for the absence of my writing. The guilt of not writing stagnated like a birdbath breeding mosquitoes. I was again strangled, captured in the grip of motherhood and desire. The metaphorical hands around my neck burned into my psyche, and I curled up. I couldn't put my feelings out into the public space. I couldn't take the chance Tom would read them. What if he used them against me, like he said he would so many times over the years? What if he actually used my own beautiful words to take Jack away from me?

I wanted an out, and I clung to anything that would justify my withdrawal. I emailed Robin with my latest attempt.

"A.J. Jacobs is a terrible blogger. His website was only updated a year ago. He's only written one blog post a year. And he's got two best-sellers." I made my argument, wholeheartedly, mind you, to Robin, as I simultaneously scanned the author's online presence. Surely this was affirmation that I wouldn't have to blog to be read, that I could skip the technology, the social media shenanigans and just go straight to the real stuff: writing a novel that could stay hidden in digital folders on my desktop.

"Who the hell is *he*?" Robin asked in reply.

"Editor-at-large for *Esquire*. Author of *Know It All* and *A Year of Living Biblically*. He's the crème de la crème, right up there with Elizabeth Gilbert." My heroes, I thought.

"Ah! That explains it. When you become editor-at-large for *Esquire*, I won't make you blog either!"

Chapter 11

Two Connors

The inherited conversations of my family linger, over decades, in a bar of soap. To this day, when I smell Zest at my grandmother's house, I hear her voice telling us about her visits to India and Spain, and her walk along the Great Wall of China. I recall the chatter exchanged between my mother and aunts while they whisked gravy over a hot stove for Thanksgiving turkey. They complained about their husbands; the men could do no right. They complained about their Welbourne stomachs (named after ancestors of women before them) that grew bigger, sticking out more and more as they got older. For decades Grandmother declared, "I must get rid of this tummy," pressing on the round lump with her hand as if it were an iron going about the job of flattening. Then she'd reach across to my plate and eat a handful of French fries.

The same words, the same eating habits, the same

routines, the same conversations bubbled up, again and again, like the soap, all blue and zesty, smelling of perfumed chemicals. As an adult, I found comfort in these repetitions, just as I did when I was seven, running around barefoot at Grandmother's beach house, catching hermit crabs and shooting pool in the basement with cousins.

Zest has been in the family for decades, at least four, and though I've moved to different states and on to Dr. Bronner's certified fair trade organic oil soaps, I'm glad that Grandmother has not. Because for a week or two each year, when I visit her and shower in the guest bath, I wash myself with memories of the old days when Granddaddy let me drive his riding lawn mower, and Uncle Johnny caught mullet in the Intracoastal with his big net, and Mom would find chalk in the tool room to draw hopscotch squares in the driveway, and all the crazy family would gather for Christmas dinner, or Easter, or Halloween when Grandmother would come to the door wearing a tall, pointy black witch cap and an ugly, green, rubber wart nose. When she cackled, I felt cozy, cherished, and at home.

Grandmother loved being the witch for her grandchildren.

She loved dancing.

She loved to travel to faraway lands.

She loved to talk about things in books, in the millions of books she read, like the drones who mate with the queen bee and die upon ejaculation.

And she loved when I called her "Grandmother."

"It sounds so distinguished," she used say.

What we didn't say, I learned, was just as powerful. We didn't talk about the anxiety disorders many of them suffered or how to manage them. We didn't talk about my grandfather being left by his mother during the Depression, the affair my grandmother believed her husband had, or my aunt's teenage anorexia.

Over the years, as my grandmother shrunk a little more, as she turned wobbly on her feet, as she stopped dying her hair, showing that gorgeous head of glistening white, Grandmother became Granny. My mother now calls her this, as do my aunts, my cousins, and my brother. I even call her this. But sometimes, I remember how she enjoyed being Grandmother, and that is what I called her when she answered the phone that sweet November day.

"Happy Birthday, Grandmother!"

"Oh, thank you! Did you hear Lizzy-bet? We are going to have two Connors." I could almost see her puckered lips squirting out the word "two" like a sputtering garden hose.

"Yes, I did."

"Jennifer is having a baby. They're naming it after your dog." She chuckled. "Do you want to talk to Jennifer?" She set the phone down without waiting for me to answer, and I heard her call my cousin's name as if she were about to break out in a song.

Had she walked through life singing her words before I knew her? I could imagine her swaying her hips like I'd seen her do a million times before, and wondered from whom in her family she'd inherited her spirit. Or did it come with old age? Would I inherit her quirkiness as I entered my later decades? Or was I already quirky? As a writer-at-heart, I felt wacky, fun even. Perhaps my grandmother was also an artist? Though the only thing I'd ever seen her create were grocery lists written on the back of envelopes.

I must have inherited my desire to write from someone. My mother "hated" writing even a birthday card, yet her sister wrote novel-length letters. My aunt, the black sheep creative writing professor, living a loner life in Montana, cranked out books she wouldn't let anyone read. I found the words "loner" and "afraid to put my work out there" inside a trunk of my own inherited conversations around writing. Those conversations tangled themselves through many layers of self doubt: I certainly didn't want to be like my aunt, anxiety-ridden, sending home ribbons her pedigree dogs won in place of turning up at Thanksgiving dinner.

If that was the writer's life, I didn't want it. My aunt had been my earliest writing role model, and I could now see, for years, I had worried my family might think I too was cuckoo should I pursue the tainted life of a writer. Cuckoo like my mother who studied drama, only to give it up for a husband and babies; literary arts were not the "practical" reason to spend a hundred grand on college. Cuckoo like her sister who hid in Montana alongside her molding manuscripts. Besides, as my father pointed out with a chalk chart drawing on my little brother's blackboard: many strive, only a very few succeed. I couldn't have them thinking I'd put my energy into an oddball pursuit, with no ribbons to show for it.

"There are many ways to be a writer, you know? You don't have to be weird. You could be an acidhead like Jack Kerouac or an alcoholic like Truman Capote or suicidal like Sylvia Plath," said the familiar inner voice that wove stories in my head. While the voice only spoke to me in my mind, I sensed it was separate from me. A guide, of sorts. A muse. I sensed its playfulness, and imagined if the muse had a physical shape and mobility, it would hang upside down on my shoulder like a monkey.

"Or," continued the muse, "you could be prolific like Stephen King."

At Robin's urging, I'd just finished reading King's book *On Writing*, in which he suggests committing to write a thousand words a day.

"Of course, you can do that, no problem!" The muse dismissed my concern before I could even think my zillion excuses. "Plus, the man takes walks in the afternoon and places his desk on the side of the room so his life is the focus. You too, could create a healthy balance. You could have it any way you like it, really."

But could I really make that commitment? Could I let go of the inherited conversations that told me "it's not practical," and writers end up alone in the woods, poor, and the subject of behind-the-back conversations at family gatherings?

What exactly do writers do, anyway? It occurred to me that committing myself to writing would mean that every breath and action would have to be that of a writer, starting with the declaration.

"Oh for fuck's sake, writers write," the monkey muse said, and then added, "They read. They research too."

Research? I thought. I had never appreciated digging through tomes to find data.

The muse continued, "Writers write and write and write, then they practice writing. Then they write. They learn about stories and the process of writing. They write some more. They get feedback from respected professionals. They write some more. They write some more. They write some more. They talk to other writers. They attend writers' conferences. They learn about the publishing industry. They write and write and write. Then they pitch their stories, they write query letters, and they send them to literary agents. They peddle their writing. Sometimes, they read their writing out loud, even to an audience of one. But mostly, they fucking write."

I'd almost forgotten I was in the middle of a call when my cousin got on the phone, interrupting my manic interaction with the muse. "We aren't copying you, I promise. We just really like the name Connor."

"Yes, yes, it's fine," I said, my head elsewhere, thinking of Stephen King's advice to write one thousand words a day. "It's a good name. Congratulations!"

We chatted a bit about I don't know what, and by the time she handed the phone back to Granny, I had a vision:

A young woman, blonde curly hair. She's been sexually abused. She lives on a lake. Held captive. By her father? Her husband? A teacher? Someone in the small town where she lives?

The image of the girl in my mind was so powerful that an idea took hold, hanging tight in a violent ocean, still vulnerable to currents, like a seahorse grasping coral.

The girl's only spoken 545 words since her fifth birthday; she keeps count. The words are all she has. She must be selective of what she says and to whom because the words can set her off. She withholds so many words, words she loved to say, but fears she can't. No matter what the school professionals say, no matter how the neighborhood kids peg her, no matter what the townspeople say, she won't budge, because she knows she will die when the one thousandth word is spoken.

"Elizabeth-y. You still there? I can't hear you."

"Yes, I'm here." I felt excited by my idea—*one thousand words, then she dies.* I was pretty sure it was an original idea; the first, cool, original story idea I'd ever had. (Until Eddie Murphy came out with a movie, but that is another story for another day.)

Why was I so nervous, then? It was only writing. It was only words. My muse had gone silent, only Granny spoke again.

"When the baby is born, you'll have to bring your dog down so the two Connors can meet each other." She snickered.

"Yes, we'll come visit. What about you? How are *you*, Grandmother?"

"Oh, I'm fine. I'm not having any babies. I'm just looking at babies." This mother of five had done her time. Her voice squeaked a little, and she whispered because her hearing aid got too loud for her when she spoke normally.

"I love you, Grandmother." I wished I could be with her to celebrate.

"I love you too, Elizabeth-y."

We hung up, and I sat for a moment. Connor, our black, furry rescue mutt, came over to lick my hand. He wanted a walk. From now on, our family would have to qualify the name Connor every time we spoke it. Connor, the dog. Connor, the baby. I sat a little while longer, uncertain what to do next, feeling totally un-pregnant.

Chapter 12

Lies

I remember the night Tom proposed over buttery garlic bread and Abruzzo penne pasta. I remember saying yes and being happy.

I remember Tom saying he loved me. I remember one morning he surprised me with champagne and strawberries because I'd said that's what life ought to be about.

I remember drywall dust settling on the carpet. His fist still clenched. Jack, two, crying from the scary, loud crunch of the broken wall. I remember shouting, clawing, a mongoose fighting for life.

I remember believing if I made him feel better about himself, he'd stop hurting me, he'd do what was best for Jack.

I remember writing a two-page letter to his family and mine, convincing them the divorce wasn't his fault, convincing them he'd done no wrong. I remember hoping they'd believed me and pleading for us all to work together to love Jack.

I remember crying and typing and hugging my knees to my chest.

Chapter 13

Mixed Doubles

I did not win the man of my dreams in sixth grade. There were two: identical twins. Michael and Adam. Tennis players, just like me. We three had earned the top lineup on our small private middle-school team. Their mamma was our coach. I always played my matches on the court next to Michael. He'd call me EB for short and gave little words of encouragement between points. My friends said he liked me. So then I, naturally, decided to like him. It would have been a perfect match, a prepubescent André Agassi and Steffi Graf love affair.

The only complication to this grand romance was that I mixed up their names. For a year, I gushed about how madly in love I was with Adam. I made little hearts with E + A inside. All the daisies in my realm were picked clean from "He loves me. He loves me not." My friends and I played the old-school game, MASH, gobs of times to determine whether we would live in a Mansion, an

Apartment, a Shack, or a House? Three kids or twenty-one? Would my best friend be Barbara Mandrell or David Hasslehoff? More often than not, after the spiral had been drawn, the number of inside lines counted, and the wrong futures crossed out, the circled answers had revealed a promising fate with a mansion and my chosen stud.

Adam was slow to act, though. Rather impatient, I decided to take action. I wrote, in the color of roses and romance from my favorite, fine ballpoint pen, a letter on college-ruled notebook paper. It read:

Dear Adam,

(I left the body of the note completely blank.)

At the bottom, I signed it:

Love, Elizabeth

Surely any true love of mine would read between the fifty vacant lines. Surely he would know what I was too afraid to say, would know just what I meant in that second to the last word, "love." Surely, he would know.

I knew when he received the letter and felt all the emotion and desire I'd poured into the note, he'd come to me and we'd finally "go out."

I remember folding the notebook paper over and over again, into a thick, rectangular package, taking my time to let the flutter in my heart linger. A friend delivered the letter for me. Then I waited. And waited. Hopeful. Like an actress about to go on stage.

The next day, our friend reported that Adam had crumpled the letter and used it to play kickball in the classroom.

Clearly, he was no André. No use spending another moment on him. I was way too powerful and way too darn pretty for him not to like me. If he couldn't see me as special, his loss. He could just jump in a lake and drown, all strangled up in the strings of his Prince racquet. That was done. Over. I went back to getting straight A's and winning tennis matches; the stuff I was good at. The stuff I could count on. The stuff that got people to like me.

About a week later, my friend who got boobs way sooner than I knew what they were, said, "I heard Michael was upset about the letter you sent to Adam."

"Really? Why?"

"Because he likes you, duh."

"Oh no! I got them mixed up."

Over ten years later as a college sophomore at the University of Boulder, Maureen and I learned the first rule of journalism: fact check. Facts, though, bored me. Made-up stories, where my imagination could choose, intrigued me much more. My choosy imagination is why, when our communications professor Bert-Something-thing-or-Other (friends with Walter Cronkite and an old-timer-CBS-correspondent who always wore a tie and told exhausting stories from the war zone) gave our class a journalism assignment to interview two people on campus, I cozied up under a shade tree and invented characters and dialogue. I don't remember what I wrote, only that a week later, Professor Bert used my story as a prize example of a job well done. From then on, I was hooked on fiction to escape the hard work of the front lines and still make the top grades. I turned all my classes into covert adventures in creativity. Maureen, on the other hand, covered actual events, quoted real people, and double-checked her work.

I wish Maureen had shown up in our sixth-grade class at Our Savior Lutheran. She would have said, "Are you sure it's Adam you like? Let's think about this first and make sure you got the right name." Yes, she would have asked those questions exactly like that: clear, but giving me the opportunity to discover the answers for myself, so I could feel a bit empowered, not like such a heel. She could have set me straight about my first marriage, too.

All the remembering made me curious about what else I was getting mixed up. What else did I think of as the truth, but really had all wrong? What truths could be rewritten, retold, imagined, cooked-up?

Chapter 14

Ten

On the morning of Jack's tenth birthday, I prepped for his party and the neighbor kid, Sam, pulled up on his bike to take the birthday boy for a ride.

"Come on back in about thirty minutes," I said, without looking up, running a vacuum back and forth over the kitchen floor.

"Yes, ma'am," Sam replied as his Southern manners dictated.

Jack walked out of the room without turning around, too excited to engage with formalities. His party would start soon; it was his day.

On the way out, I heard him ask his friend, "Why do you think people say 'eeeww' when they see people kissing in the movies. I don't get it. And then they don't say 'eeeww' when they see someone kissing a dog."

The door slammed behind them, and I continued cleaning. From cobwebbed corners of memory, I revisited my son's birth. At one-thirty-ish on a cold afternoon in March, nurses in blue shuffled around doing I-have-no-idea-what and became white noise. My midwife asked if I wanted an incision to help him come out.

"No." I really didn't. "Let's keep pushing."

Daddy Tom barely looked up. He stood to the side, half filming the birth, half watching hockey on the TV, unavailable for comment.

"Give me your hand," said the midwife. She guided my sweaty fingers down to the opening where a little human being emerged. "Can you feel him?"

Oh my god, I could! I caressed the top of his head, malleable, soft, fuzzy, wet, a ripe peach; I couldn't believe I actually felt his head coming out of my root chakra. Tom would alternate between holding my hand, filming Jack's head, and tracking the Red Wings score.

My pushing was rewarded. I earned an A+, the most important one. Eight minutes later, he'd fully arrived through no incision, into the dry, physical world, extending head to toe the length of one of my writing notebooks. His nose came out crooked and bloody from the journey down the birth canal. Dad paid attention at that point, documenting embryonic fluids. I lay still in bed, amazed, glad for the team that had guided me step-by-step on how to push and breathe and deliver a human being. Doctors and nurses disposed of the embryonic sac and wiped up goo while I lay, drugged, detached, disconnected from my birthing power as a woman, yet thanking God that I didn't have to give birth naturally: squatting and hallucinating from pain.

Oohing and ahhing, the nurses took our baby to a table in the side room and lay him on his back. Jack screamed in staccatos (perhaps foreshadowing a future in the marching band?) and peed in a straight shot to the ceiling. Tom caught that on film, too.

It didn't take long for the novelty of a newborn to wear off and Tom to invoke his "pass" card. After only a few weeks, he declined to take part in night-time feedings, demanded he have time to himself, and played a daily rerun of "I've worked all day, I need to rest, I shouldn't have to deal with the baby when I get home." He left Jack either predominantly in my care, in front of the TV, or pawned off into the arms of loving grandparents.

As I prepped for Jack's tenth birthday party and reminisced, in chronological order, from the first months into the first few years of Jack's life, I felt the flinching in my belly of what had come next—hands around my throat, fists punching holes in drywall, and the constant threat to take my son away if I didn't do what Tom wanted. Like each time before, I forced those memories into mental filing cabinets I didn't open.

Instead, I focused on the surprised rapidness of ten years gone by. Just like that.

I had scheduled an appointment to have the IUD removed, but made no plans to get another one just yet. I waffled between wanting another child and freedom; no way did I want to wait another two continuous decades of putting their needs in front of my own while I, energy-less, skipped out on adult socials, African safaris, and long, luxurious stretches with my head in a story, typing slower than the ideas came.

The comparison of life with a baby versus life without occupied me as I finished vacuuming the rest of the house and moved to sweeping the front porch. I enjoyed being on the stoop, in daylight, present to green philodendrons perking up from the previous night's spring rain and the decadent warmth of my body like a marshmallow in the sun. I brushed away dead lizard tails, compared the pros and cons of life with and without a baby, then swept grits of sand, then compared, swept, compared, swept, compared, then heard Jack and Sam laughing and shouting from bike to bike as they road up the street.

I admired my son: a big boy now, nose straightened out, the brown hair on his head smooth and dry like rayon. Sam called out, "See you later" as he whizzed home. Jack bumped his front tire over the sidewalk and rode straight into the grass, jumping off in one continuous motion, so even the bike stood upright for a moment before it realized its rider was done. As the bike plopped to the grass, stiff on its side, Jack ran up to me.

"It doesn't have to be perfect," he said.

"*Yeah, it doesn't have to be perfect*," repeated the distant voice of the echo muse.

Addicted to "just one more edit," I pushed the remaining leaves off the porch with another few sweeps.

Jack grabbed the broom from my hand. "Mom, enough working. There's fun to be had."

Chapter 15

Rain

Indeed, after Jack had his fun, I went to the laptop for mine.

I remember rain I typed into the blog post. It fell on my head and made my hair stick to my eyes and neck. I didn't care. I held his hand. We quick-walked, slopping in our shoes through the streets of New Orleans. The downpour dulled the colors of the city, but I couldn't see any way behind the glaze of desire. I was wet, inside and out. Only five more blocks to go before my saturated body would be rumbling as violently as the thunder, pouring out all the condensation that had built up for the last thirty years.

A short, crisp ditty. I hit "publish" on Wordpress.

Rain, I scribbled the word on a blank sheet of paper, in elegant cursive, letting my hand feel the looping of the letter "r" and ending with the tail of the "n."

Rain. The writer's metronome.

I traced over the letters again and again.

I was filled up.

I pliéd myself to the kitchen to refill a cup of tea.

"Gabe?" I swiped a kiss across the back of his blond head as he pulled carrots, an onion, and chicken from the fridge to cook a post-birthday party dinner.

"Yes, darling?"

"I *do not* want any more children. If I tell you otherwise, don't believe me."

Chapter 16

Six Rocks

Six rocks sat on my writing desk: two came from my grandmother's beach in Florida, two from mountain hikes in Colorado, and two from Gomera in the Canary Islands, my first exotic getaway with Gabe. The smallest rock was pebble-like, about the circumference of a quarter, and white with a wispy, but clearly defined, black circle that wrapped around the stone like a wedding band. Another was perfectly round, perfectly smooth, perfect except for the coffee-stained birthmark that covered a curved edge. In contrast was a chip from the Colorado Rockies, jagged with green splotches that could be mistaken for what I imagine might be Leprechaun vomit. Another rock reminded me of Saturn with layers of thin rings in varying shades of sand.

Originally, I'd placed them on my desk, close by, so I could touch them when I felt scared or blank or the need for connection to powerful moments. Connection would help, I thought. Connection to the earth. Connection to my center, wherever that is. But I never touched the stones once, except to reposition them after Jack's backpack had landed on my desk, knocking them out of place.

To the left of the rocks, and a little further toward the top corner of the desk, rested a vase: a yellow, curvy structure with a base expanding outwards in the width and shape of an oversized, luxurious tea cup, then coming back together at the top in a pinch of round opening, trimmed with a thick circular strip of red. I liked the opening outlined in red, a squirt of blood against a belly pregnant with sunshine.

As I wrote, the vase held water and the sprig of a viburnum branch leaning to the side. The glossy, forest green leaves suggested a postcard of a palm leaf in the rain. Tropical. Alive. Reminding me to find the keys and get on out the door: there's a whole world to see.

Which got me thinking. . . .

Where in the world did the girl live? I wondered. The girl I'd seen in my vision, the fictional character whose story was taking shape in my imagination. I felt her presence with me constantly, as if she were real, riding in the backseat with Jack as I dropped him off to school or hovering over me while Gabe and I made love. She consumed my thoughts as I mapped out the pieces of her life, getting bits and insights from things I'd see around town or conversations in passing, like the one I had with my friend who described an out-of-body experience she'd had one night as a child in which she had hovered over her bed.

I'm often surprised by what it takes for people to

survive, children even more. And yet they do. I wanted to understand why a father might abuse his daughter sexually, why a mother would not say anything about it, why a daughter would still love her abuser, and how that little girl could go on in the face of such trauma. How could I create characters that the reader would connect with despite their flaws? How could I tell a story combining abuse and love in the same breath?

While I sought answers, the character, abused and resilient and fearing death as she tracked the words she spoke, bravely charged ahead in my mind. She was a trickster, that one, and she cursed like a motherfucker, to herself, of course, because she couldn't say "fuck," "asshole," or "shit" out loud. Not yet, anyway. At night, she would leave her body, hover above her bed as if in a dream, and imagine a padlocked door below to protect her sleeping physical form.

The ideas trickled in, beginning to make a whole. I felt the pull in my belly, wanting to put her story to paper, wanting to find her words.

Do you think I could birth a novel out of this vase? I reflected, wondering if that rogue muse was in the vicinity. I waited for an answer, admiring the long, lanky candle burning to my right. The thinnest line of wax dripped down the side, forming little humps, a miniature dragon's tail.

What if I *could* birth a novel?

Six rocks sat firm, unwavering in their commitment to ground me, word by word, no matter how off-centered I felt, and a cunning muse echoed, "What if? What if? What if?"

Chapter 17

Mad

The moment a teaspoon of possibility arrives, resistance enters like an FBI house raid. I'm not sure why resistance likes to create a disturbance capable of forcing one into prescription drugs. Maybe to create drama? A plot point? To make artists prove they want it, can do it? Or just to mess around like a monkey muse? Whatever the reasons, resistance never ends. I'm still learning how to ignore its many disguises including (but definitely not limited to) an unmade bed, moving house, to-do lists, grocery shopping, a napping-couch, a headache, yeah-buts, adopting a new puppy, and hurt feelings, like on the day I found out Maureen was pregnant.

"Oh! My! God!" I hadn't realized I'd yelled it until I heard Gabe calling from the other room, "What's the matter, sweetie?"

I slammed up from my chair, yanked the cord out of the laptop and carried it, an open book.

"Here," I said, shoving my entire computer into Gabe's lap before he could open up a *New York Times.* "Read it." My pointy finger stuck straight out, tapping hard as if I could hammer the email through the screen and force the message back to sender.

He looked down, scanning his eyes over the letter.

"Out loud, please." My tone was not polite.

Gabe read: *"Hi Elizabeth, are you coming to Denver for Maureen's baby shower? I'm trying to get a head count. Also, if you have any ideas on games we could play, I'd love to hear them. Maybe even a song or a dance? Love, Sara Jane."*

Gabe looked up. "Who's Sara Jane?"

Eyes rolled, I put my hands on my hips. "Sister-in-law. That is not the point!"

"I didn't know Maureen was having a baby."

"Exactly." I yanked the computer from his lap and stomped back to my desk.

I sat on the edge of my seat, fingers curved, writhing over the keyboard but not touching a single key. I wiggled my fingers fast. I couldn't wait to pounce on the keys, pushing into them hard, with all my fury. Only, I didn't know what words to write. Emotions swirled: anger, confusion, fear. Had she secretly downgraded our friendship status without telling me?

A baby shower!?

Confusion provoked anxiety which provoked questions I couldn't answer, questions that made no sense. If she didn't tell me, then maybe she didn't even really want me to attend her baby shower? Wasn't it only a week ago we last spoke? Maybe two weeks? It seemed so recent, but maybe I hadn't called in a while; I didn't recall the time passing. Maureen didn't like when we'd go long stretches without talking. Regardless, that's no reason to send a best friend to the weed eater. Maureen must have a good reason for not telling me this, she must. How could my best friend not tell me she was p-r-e-g-n-a-n-t?

I felt mad. Left out. Hurt. Mad. Real mad. Shock settled in like an ice cube in bourbon. So I typed:

Hey, way to tell your best friend you're pregnant. Did you put me back in the doghouse?

Too pissy, I decided.

How about, *Wow, you're pregnant. Should I pretend I still don't know?*

Which brought up a good point. Should I?

Maybe Maureen was waiting to tell me in person. Maybe Sara Jane was just a type A baby shower planner and had sent out invites before Maureen could spread the good news. I mean, maybe Maureen had been trying to call me all day, and I just hadn't answered my phone because I'd been off working and daydreaming about how I could come up with the money to buy a new Mac-Book Pro. Yes, that was it.

I checked the cell, but none of the day's calls were from Maureen. I even scrolled through the call history for the last week. Somewhere there must have been a missed call? A rogue voice mail? A carrier pigeon? But no.

We were going to be pregnant together, opening packages

with hand-woven blankets and booties while eating Jell-O, I thought.

I didn't eat Jell-O, of course. I didn't even buy Jell-O. When I was eight, still losing baby teeth and convinced I would do grown-up way better than Mom and Dad, I figured Jell-O would be on every grocery list. As an adult, fabulous or not, my pantry contained brown rice, lentils, quinoa. I even bought organic dog biscuits. I barely remembered what I'd liked about Jell-O, a goofy food. With a mind of its own, Jell-O didn't stay put. Jell-O seemed to laugh a lot, usually at the human about to eat it. Then again, Jell-O could be still and quiet. Observing, placid. Drenched in red. Or green. Or pink. Jell-O picked a side and stuck with it. No changing colors mid-term. It was what it was. Mostly, Jell-O didn't seem to have a problem being Jell-O. I'd rather like to be Jell-O. I thought if I were more like Jell-O, maybe Maureen would love me again.

I kicked up out of my chair for the third time, knocking it backward.

"Gabriel?!" I barreled through, a warning horn on a train. "Maureen is pregnant."

The *Times*, unfolded in his hands, stood as a wall between him and me, a metaphor for the barriers seemingly constructed since I had started asking about babies and marriage.

"Yes, I know. That's really great," he said from behind his great wall, The Great Wall of New York Gabriel Times.

"She didn't tell me." I practically bit at him through the paper. I would make him remove that divide between us, even if I had to sneak that paper into the food processor and mince it into a frothy broth.

He breathed in, then folded the *Times* along its appropriate seams, gently laying it on the floor.

"Come here," he said, tender, patting his chest, encouraging me to crawl inside his arms and nuzzle up to his heart, safe and warm, cradled like an embryo. He offered me love to feed on until I was ready to go back into the big, cold, Maureen-message-less world. Once I knew he was willing to console me as I broke down over Maureen's big news, I found the strength to fight.

"I've got to go write to her."

"Don't make it mean so much. She loves you," he shouted to my backside.

Back at the ol' slowing MacBook, I deleted the *Wow, you're pregnant . . . should I pretend I don't know?* comment and rubbed my chin with my forefinger, wondering how many others had been cheated out of knowing their best friend was pregnant.

M-a-u-r-e-e-n, I wrote, seething still. *I'd love to come to your baby shower. Thank you for the invitation.*

Then I added, for a touch of jagged humor, *By the way, are you pregnant?*

I almost hit send, but paused instead.

Maybe she really did want to tell me? Maybe I should let her? I didn't want to be a passive-aggressive fuck. My breathing slowed for a moment, and I remembered the day she'd introduced herself to me, so kind, smiling, with her long, curly hair. Some people ask, "How are you?" merely as protocol; she'd asked me like she really wanted to know.

"Okay," I said to the ceiling, saving the draft. "I'll give her a week."

Chapter 18

Carpool

Birds had crapped quarter-sized gobs of dark-brown and speckled-white mini-logs on the expansive white hood of the '97 Mercury Marquis I'd inherited from my other grandmother when she passed away. I noticed them as Gabe, Jack, Connor-the dog-not-my-cousin's-baby, and I sat in the car line waiting to drop Jack off at school.

"Do you have a coupon for a color copy, Mommy?" Jack asked me the question from his usual backseat ride.

I didn't hear it, didn't answer, just stared at the bird shit on the hood.

What will the schoolteachers tending the car line think? Will they say I'm a bad mother, dirty, not fit to raise a child? Maybe it's more than a sign I shouldn't have babies; maybe I should definitely move out of state? And I'll probably have to seriously reconsider my relationship. I mean, maybe this is just a big ol' sign that Gabe and I aren't right for each other anymore. And, my God, how many birds does it really take to do this kind of poop job? What does it mean that Maureen hasn't called and I have all this shit on my car? Is it a metaphor for the sewage-like nature of life? My life?

The muse chimed in, "Metaphor my monkey ass! Run it through a damn car wash."

Maybe if I hadn't done that thing in college, that thing we can't talk about, maybe then I would be making a higher salary. Or I'd have sold a novel. Oh dear God, I'm definitely going to have to go shopping. Maybe if I have nicer clothes, the birds will like me and shit on Gabe's mini-van instead.

"Poop! Poop! Poop!" The monkey muse danced in my head while Jack shouted from the back seat.

"M-o-o-o-o-m! Do . . . you . . . have . . . a . . . coupon . . . for . . . a . . . color . . . copy?

Then again, maybe the shit on my car is really just shit. Maybe my goo-ridden car just means that some birds sat on a tree branch all night eating berries, worms and whatever else birds eat; then they took a community dump.

"Mom!"

"Sorry, baby. I was distracted. I'm present now. What did you say?"

"Oh, never mind." He rolled his eyes, glassy from sleep.

Oh God, I wasn't listening to my child. What does that mean? What will Jack think? Will he need therapy for the rest of his life? Does he think I'm a bad mother? Not fit to raise a child? I should definitely move out of state. Does Gabe really love me?

"Have a great day at school today," Gabe said as he pulled the car up to the entrance.

"Look for miracles today," I said, positivity on overkill, unsure if I was trying to inspire him or me.

"There are no miracles at school, Mom," Jack corrected, clearly irritated, as he forced himself out of the car, red backpack slumping his shoulders. The bell rang; Jack jumped to attention, slammed the car door, and rushed off.

"He's a cutie. It's tough growing up," Gabe said, shifting the car into drive.

I rolled down the back windows so Connor-the dog-not-baby could suck in the fresh air, while I contemplated having babies or not.

A couple of days had gone by and still no word from Maureen, which was exactly why I should not have wanted to have another baby. How could Maureen and I raise our kids together, side by side, like sisters, if she doesn't even tell me she's having a baby?

But there was much more to my indecision: I could feel myself slowing. I liked to sleep in. And through the night. I also liked naps, and reading quietly in a chair, undisturbed. With each year Jack aged, I became less and less interested in planning Spring Flings at under-attended PTO meetings, playing catch in the street, or jumping up and down like we used to when Jack was a toddler and a fire truck passed.

Plus, I recognized the irony of talking babies while in a rough patch. Shouldn't there be a warning label? Don't be thinking about getting pregnant at the same time you are pricing antidepressants.

Stranger still, I was beginning to see a pattern that

I could not—would not—admit to anyone: I seemed to want babies the most when I felt unhappy, unfulfilled, and unsatisfied. Perhaps, just perhaps, during a depression is not the best time to pop a little Joey into my pouch, for the hospital has a "no return" policy and won't refund the charge.

Despite all the reasons not to, I just couldn't get the feeling gone. "Let's have babies," I blurted out to Gabe.

He slowed the car to a stop at the sign at the end of the road and rubbed the top of his forehead, ruffling the blond bush of his Christopher Lloyd brows. "Can we talk about this later?"

"Why don't you want to have kids with me?" I knew the question wore him out.

"Why is it so important to you? Why do you want to have a baby?" he asked.

"You never answer my question."

I could see him thinking, really thinking. Not once had he ever answered a question of mine (no matter what topic) with sheer and utter abandon. The methodical engineering with which he constructed his thoughts earned my trust. Without his planning and focus, we would be a pinball machine. Yet, I wanted him to be wild. Just once.

"Well," he started, "For one, the less responsibility the better. I want us to have more freedom to travel and have adventures. Two, I don't really have the headspace for a baby right now. I'm focused on completing my business projects so we can move on. I can't afford anything that would distract me. Thirdly, while I'm optimistic in general, my worldview of the macroeconomics has not changed, and I think that in the next decade, it will be difficult enough without adding extra worry. We have Jack to look after."

"So you are saying that you don't *ever* want to have children with me?"

"Baby, we *have* a child. We are raising a child, already."

My God, did I find his priorities irritating. *The birds definitely better shit on his car.*

He rubbed his eyes again with one hand on the steering wheel and licked the corner of his lips like he was looking for water. "So, why is it important to you to have a baby?"

"Because it just is" seemed like a perfectly acceptable response to me, but I knew he wouldn't take the bait. I would have to first think of an answer to inspire him to act, to counter his reasoning, but besides the bird shit, all I could think about was coffee.

I don't drink coffee. I wish I did; I could use a hit of caffeine. The burnt toast taste is too bitter for me to ingest, but I do love the smell. Coffee grounds are rich, earthy. They make a home smell lived in, weathered like a Western saddle. When the fear of an unknown I can't distinguish has tangled me captive in my own bed, the coffee grounds bring me into the world. I can practically feel the waves of aroma holding my hand, reminding me I am safe. The water percolates and drips into the pot, warm, flavorful, inviting me over. It laughs a little. "Are you sure you don't want to have me?" the brew teases.

Yes, indeed, I was sure I didn't like coffee. The more rejected I felt by Gabe and the more suspicious I became over Maureen's silence, the more exhilarating it felt to be sure about something. I used to get so excited about trips to Europe or speaking engagements on radio shows or a weekend training course or moving into a new home. As uncertainty crept in at work, in love, in friendship, and in myself, I found that in order to "be normal" I *had* to be stoked when I showered in the morning. I *forced* myself to celebrate in the basic necessities of life and the simple mundane truths like the flame of a burning candle, the fraying toothbrush on my sink, and the profound knowing that I did not like the taste of coffee. If I didn't embrace that knowing, I wasn't sure I would survive the twisted spat of psychological winter.

Gabe kept on driving, and I couldn't remember if Maureen drank coffee. After fifteen years of friendship, surely I must know her preference. I've heard it said our brains are so powerful that our memory bank stores even the information we only hear once; we'll know it forever. According to this theory, I could, hypothetically, speak Spanish fluently.

The practical application of my entire four years of learning, however, translated into *"Dónde está la playa?"* Frankly, "Where is the beach?" did not qualify me to be a Hispanic diplomat, or even a *camarero* at the local bar. Whatever study found that my brain knows everything it has ever encountered needed to also provide the 800 number to the locksmith, so I could have someone come over right away to jimmy rig the portal. Then, I could know whether I ought to offer Maureen coffee or tea next time I saw her. *If* I ever saw her again.

Did it make me a terrible friend that I didn't remember her caffeine preferences? Was my forgetfulness the reason she hadn't yet told me about the bun in the oven?

I hoped not; I loved her and all the hours it takes for her to apply sunscreen before she will go outside. I loved her when she didn't return my call for weeks. I loved her even if I didn't see her for months. When it came to Maureen and me, the measure of time seemed so inadequate, like pound cake.

Why hasn't she called to tell me?

Why do I want a baby, when Gabriel does not? To prove him wrong? To prove he really did want kids with me (an expression of our unified love) after all? Because Jack will someday not want to snuggle? Because, if it's a girl, she will have blond curls like her daddy? Because a child must love his mamma? Because I want to be loved best of all?

"Get a kitten!" the monkey muse, unsympathetic as usual, butted in.

Because, if he wanted to have a baby with me, then I'd have a purpose?

If he loved me enough he'd just do it, I thought.

I slumped in the passenger seat. Arms folded. Teeth gritted. Gabe drove home, next to me, his eyes gentle, trying so hard to find the key to unhook the baby-wanting padlock clasped to my armor.

For a couple of years, we had a lot of those third-grade moments. I'm not proud of them, but I didn't know how else to respond. Years later, I would recognize the spotty self-love and the grip that lived around my neck, and I would find the answers to my questions. Back then, I only felt desperation.

I looked at him, squinting my eyes. His mouth was still, no remnants of words, no evidence he'd say anything more, just waiting patiently for me to respond to his ever-question "why?"

"Just because," I answered at last.

Chapter 19

Of Course Happy

"John and Jayda called," Gabe said later that night while frying onions for spaghetti sauce, a dishtowel draped over his left shoulder. I admired his thick bicep as he lifted the frying pan from the burner to shuffle the onions. He'd gained some weight over the past few months, and his belly stuck out over his jeans, but I loved that belly, rubbing it for luck every chance I got.

"How are they?" I asked, remembering the sweetness of being in his arms as I attempted to move through another gray patch. He'd learned not to "fix it" anymore. Instead he'd hold me and say simple words like, "Just cry. It's okay. I'm strong enough for both of us." His chest, when I snuggled up to it, felt inflated, hardened, packed-full of the unspoken. At times, as he held me, I caught him staring up at the corner of the ceiling, looking just as lost, just as unsure as I felt.

"They're getting married," he said, adding ground meat to the pan and sending up plumes of smoke and steam.

"Great, when's the wedding?" A trip to Malibu might be the perfect reset button. I'd bring my fleece and wooly hat for walks on the beach to watch dolphins surf. We could drive down to Abbot Kinney for the day, hold hands, and window shop for eclectic items to help me remember that I'm of the world, not just this small town in the South. While there, I'd pop into the Hard Tail store and pick up a new yoga top. Maybe we'd lollygag along the boardwalk in Venice Beach and see if we could spot anyone famous or tripping on acid. I wondered what was playing at the theaters on the Strip? God, even the *thought* of city life felt invigorating.

"Not sure," he answered, focusing on the sauce. "But, they're also pregnant."

I walked out of the kitchen without a word.

Of course, I was happy for John and Jayda. I was happy for all the goddamn pregnant people.

Chapter 20

Unsinkable

When Maureen finally called a week later, I answered the phone thinking about a seventy-degree, sunny Colorado day in May when our twenty-year-old bodies had pedaled bicycles up a mountain. I remembered how Maureen rode the bike like my mother rode a horse: at ease, with command. Just the slightest shift of her thigh, and the bike would take off up an incline. Steady. Consistent. Effortless.

Two hundred yards behind her, I huffed. My feet pedaled in fast bursts just to catch up. But I never could. I'd stop every hundred yards, exhaling in quick, sharp gusts like an airport security puffer machine. My legs ached and protested every yard, my knees boycotted each spin of the wheel, my thighs wrote resignation letters with each turn. When I came to the same incline Maureen had zipped up, I popped off my seat and walked. Again and again, I pedaled fast to catch up, then tuckered out.

Fifteen years after our bike ride in Glenwood Canyon, waiting for Maureen's explanation of "not telling the best friend about the baby," I still puffed. I felt frantic and hysterical, pedaling through life just to catch up to the steady human kindness, openness, and acceptance Maureen embodied for me. Just out of college, she had introduced me to Tori Amos at a Red Rocks concert where the music swallowed me just like the little earthquakes Amos writes about and awakened me to lyrics and thoughts and ideas that catapulted me out of my childhood Disney cocoon into the real world. One year, she had planned a birthday surprise for me at the Molly Brown House Museum because, at some point that I don't remember, I'd mentioned that I loved watching Debbie Reynolds dance and kick her heels in *The Unsinkable Molly Brown*. During my first marriage, when Maureen caught Tom shouting at me, "You should be happy to be married to me. I don't beat you," she took the edge off, comforted me, and distracted me. After Hurricane Katrina destroyed my home, Maureen had flown to Louisiana, then driven with me, Jack, and our surviving books, photo albums, and clothes to Colorado, to hunker down and figure out what do to next. Years of friendship deeds dotted my memory as I listened to her on the other end of the phone, trying so hard to make it right.

"I'm sorry," Maureen said, sounding every bit the thousands of miles away that she lived. Though both knew our distance was no longer measured by the expanse over mountains. It was now measured in the age gap of my son to her unborn child, my preference for variety versus her comfort in structure, and metaphors like the size of our wrists. Her wrist is solid, a persisting difference, a forever physical reminder that she is she, and I am I. She can wear a bangle bracelet like no other. My wrist is too bony. I get lost in a bangle, overpowered, like a forest choked by kudzu. Maureen, like her wrist, was solid in life. She'd built a clientele over years, lived in the same house for years, religiously set aside money in a retirement account, and exfoliated her lips every night with a toothbrush. I, on the other hand, lived my life as if being chased. I dashed from job to job, moved from state to state, spent money before I made it, and prided myself on the fact that eating was the only routine thing I did every day. I liked the adventure of not knowing what came next. Maureen always knew.

"I really wanted to tell you. But I wanted to do it in person and was hoping we could talk on the phone," she said. Another measure that gapped us: Maureen needed talking. I would have happily engaged with a written "I'm prego!" in a quick email or a text.

"Our lives are so different," Maureen sighed, speaking what I had been thinking. "What do we have in common anymore? Sometimes, I wonder why you even like me. You've grown so much. I haven't."

If I had grown, Maureen had something to do with it. In her eyes, I'd learned about being a friend. I'd learned to be steadier. I'd learned to show up when she expected me to. In the quarreling times, I had learned to feel safe in our friendship despite our differences because I knew we'd work it out, no matter what. I knew she wasn't like the man who put his hands on my neck. From her, I'd learned that we don't walk away simply because we are different. She made me want to be a better friend; I didn't want to disappoint her. I wanted to be the friend she could count on as much as I had counted on her over the years.

I was angry at the hands I still felt around my neck. I kept running from those hands. Tom's hands. Teachers' hands. My parents' hands. All the hands that I thought were trying to choke out self-expression, make me someone else, someone they wanted me to be. As I began to see how I was conditioned to feel betrayal, to look for evidence of betrayal more than support, I became aware that I was not angry with Maureen at all. Maureen had never asked me to be anyone but me. She loved me when I was grumpy. She loved me when I was sad. She loved me when I flaked on her. She loved me. Period.

"I never should have married Tom," I thought out loud.

She laughed. "You know I wanted to slap you when you told me you two got engaged."

"Why didn't you?"

"You wouldn't have listened to me."

She was probably right. I'd had to learn my own lessons then, just as I had to learn them now.

"Can you come to the baby shower? I really want you there," she begged.

"Yes, of course, I'll come," I replied. Our differences didn't matter. What mattered was our commitment as friends. And, Maureen is a *real* friend, the kind that embodies the entire world of the word and all the letters and spaces inside it. And this was exactly the kind of friend I needed as I spent those days leafing through six huge binders of happy-making solutions I'd learned from years of self-help seminars, searching for the magic formula to keep me sane in the tug-of-war between babies and writing. I was told once to be sweet on myself, but I didn't trust myself to be sweet then. I'd gotten so used to running from the hands around my neck, running from myself, running from writing, running and afraid. I still puffed. I felt frantic and hysterical; I looked to Maureen, a bangle of sweetness.

"I still can't believe you are actually pregnant." I glanced around my little nook of an office, taking in the contour of the brick floor and a sprinkle of Mississippi rat poop. A faint *tick-tock* hummed in my brain like the motor of a refrigerator where I could keep eggs chilled, waiting for the right time, waiting for the day Gabe said yes.

"I'm so sorry," she continued; I heard the regret in her voice.

I trusted that regret. I trusted her to love me even when I screwed up.

I could count on Maureen like I could count on stone.

"It's okay. I'm over it." Then I added, "You know, I don't love you because we are the same. I love you because it's you. We've come this far, and I'm not going anywhere."

We both sat for a moment in the saccharine pause of relief.

"So, is it a boy or a girl?" I asked.

Meanwhile, the monkey muse whispered in my ear: *What if you had the conviction of Stephen King to write at least a thousand words, no matter what? Night after night? Year after year? Doubt after doubt?* My muse tilled the tale about that ten-year-old with blonde ringlets who could only speak a thousand words before she dies. When Maureen hung up, I quickly opened a blank word document to capture the scenes and bits of dialogue. A novel began. And I felt happy.

Chapter 21

No Vacancy

Two weeks after Maureen and I made up, I could not remember the sex of her unborn child. Just like I forgot whether or not she drank coffee.

Gabe was no help. "Why don't you just call and ask her?"

"I can't. She's told me several times. I'd look like an idiot. And a *very bad* friend."

I worried I would make the wrong move with Maureen, with Gabe, with Jack, with my life. I worried I wouldn't have a baby ever again. I worried I would regret not having a baby again. I worried so much about what to do that I'd bitten my nails down to short, stubby, jagged, frayed quicks.

I'd tried all the nail-biting tricks before: oil cuticle massages, once-a-week manicures, and moisturizing my hands at night and wrapping them in socks. But when worry set in, when I struggled with decisions, when I didn't know where to turn, when babies occupied my mind, no aid could save my helpless phalanges.

I chewed through Essie's Devil's Advocate.

I chewed through Bitter Nails, no matter how awful tasting.

I chewed on the bold extremes.

Nails. No nails.

Baby. No baby.

Write. No write.

Gabe. No Gabe.

Want. No want. Want again.

These contradictions swelled inside me, leaving no room to grow anything else. Which was why Gabe and I escaped for the day from our little bayside town to New Orleans. Sans Jack, we remembered what we'd talked about before we talked about babies: traveling to Mallorca, modern architecture, German movies, fine wines. We remembered walking hand in hand, a simple couple with nowhere to go, no school lunch to pack, no budget to balance, no "shoulds" to manage, no battles to win. Just windows luring us with objects to glide our hands over, colored trinkets to fuel our imaginations, rich fabrics woven into sundresses, suits, camisoles, jeans, and lingerie to distract me from the ruckus in my head, the unease in my throat.

The New Orleans heat rose from the asphalt, unwelcome. Despite the sweat, my arms felt at home wrapped around Gabe's. I didn't want to take my hand away ever. Even as I questioned our opposing desires and whether Gabe and I should continue on, I loved him. If I did move on for a man who wanted a baby, maybe I'd end up somewhere truly dreadful, with only a Wal-Mart, where we would never touch interesting objects or window shop. Maybe I would never find my way out.

Despite my doubts, that day in New Orleans altered something in me, and I felt a bud of hope sprouting in my heart.

"Let's go in there." I steered us into the Bath and Body Works on Magazine Street; maybe they sold a new nail product I could try.

Inside, round barrels dotted the showroom and over-flowed with pretty pink soaps, loofahs, moisturizers, and scented candles. Gabe and I unlinked ourselves and sla-lomed through the shop. I squirted a glob of peppermint lotion from a tester bottle into my hand, feeling refreshed from the tingling. Then I covered the scent with a glob from another tester. Tangerine this time. Yum. After the third tester, I could no longer distinguish the smells. Lavender, lilac, grapefruit, rose, coffee, dandelion—all bounced off each other, creating confusion and chaos like the boiling molecules of choices that had left me feeling disoriented and lost, no vacancy for tracking a plot line or even the sex of my best friend's baby.

Whether from the scent of competing perfumes or the drudgery of tangled choices, my head began to hurt. But I wasn't ready to leave the store. I spotted nailbrushes that I could use to scrub my jagged cuticles. And, where there were pumice stones, a foot massage must be in my future. I could use a foot massage.

"Can I help you?" the clerk asked, her eye lashes

clumped from thick mascara. I was tempted to reach over to her and smooth them out with my fingertips.

"No, thank you. I'm just looking."

Gabriel whistled to me from across the room, holding up a jar of foot scrub. I could tell he was having the same dreamy thoughts of massage. Maybe we could go home, have a footbath, and apply a mud mask while our feet soaked. Seemed easy enough, and my therapy had taught me to make simple things the cornerstones of my day. I really was working hard to create anchors that I could cling to among the writer's negative self talk: "This sucks," "What's the point?" and "No one really cares."

The self-loathing seemed to come naturally like the mole on my chest. But I didn't believe I was simply stranded atoms of self-doubt, impossible to shape-shift, left to rot. Surely, somewhere inside of me, I had a well of strength, power, confidence, clarity, and self-love. The trouble was, I hadn't yet learned how to access it, so I picked up ten-dollar knick-knacks, nail brushes, and lavender lotions for a quick hit of self-Sweet'n Low.

Gabe, as usual, answered his ringing cell phone.

"Hallo. Wie geht's?"

I eavesdropped while I contemplated whether to buy the mint or tangerine body lotion. Though I didn't understand the words he spoke, I could tell by the tenderness in his voice and the goofy laugh that he was talking to his best friend, Ferdie, probably telling dirty jokes. Gabe walked to the other side of the store seemingly in another world.

Ferdie and Gabe had grown up together in Dort-mund, Germany, where they'd placed in bubble gum blowing contests, tipped cows, and unhitched railroad cars in the cover of night. They were never far from skinny-dipping or trespassing (or whatever "trouble"). Gabe is the worrywart, the judge, and the lookout. Ferdie is the instigator, which is why his landing in Arizona had surprised me, as Phoenix was not a place to insti-gate anything. It's a place to survive, a treeless gladiator arena of rattlesnakes, maniac drivers, shriveled skin, and vegetation as grating as the sun. I had been there a few weeks earlier on a work trip, and had stuck closely to the air-conditioning, misting machines, and mall. I hadn't whined a bit when Ferdie and his girlfriend, Josie, took me to a generic Starbucks to relax between shopping and sightseeing.

It was in that chain cafe, sipping tea, months before I found out Maureen was pregnant, that Ferdie gave me advice I couldn't get out of my mind:

"I know Gabe," he had said. "I know how he works. The more you push him, the more you bring up the sub-ject, the more he'll turn away. If you want a baby, you should have one. But you won't change his mind by asking him all the time. If you want it that badly then you will probably have to break up with him. Maybe he would decide that it's not worth it and come back. But maybe not."

"So your advice is to break up with him?"

"Yes." He paused. "If you really want a baby."

His words hardened like concrete in my gut. I thought

of them day and night. I thought of them while showering, frying onions, biting my nails, and sitting on the john. And I thought of them in the Bath and Body Works on Magazine Street, while Gabe rattled off something in German and the clerk watched me from under her umbrella of mascara.

I suddenly wondered what the point was of being in this store, sneezing lilac and vanilla. The future seemed so predictable. Clearly, I wasn't going to buy anything for myself. We were not going to make that footbath. We would not be mixing mud masks. Something always got in the way. Phone calls. Time. Inertia. Apathy. History would repeat itself; I could see the future as clearly as I could see my toes, all the way down past my flat, embryo-less belly.

Oblivious, Gabe gabbed away in a corner surrounded by pastel loofahs, and I walked over to the rack of greeting cards wishing that just once in my life I could act like a character in a movie, say something obnoxious, and stomp out of the store. If I could just move beyond the hurdle to speak and write freely. If I could say something new, *anything* I hadn't said before, it would be a start. A good start.

As I racked my brain for a movie character and stomp-out exit line, I picked up a white greeting card with the simple image of a yellow rubber duck and got an idea. My eyes darted around the store until . . . bingo! I found what I was looking for in the barrel right under my nose.

"Gabe!" I waved to him, indicating he had to come to me right now.

He said what sounded like a cheery goodbye to the German on the other end and did my bidding.

"Yes, darling?" He kissed me. I would miss those kisses if I left, but I couldn't think of that now. I was saved from the humiliation of admitting to Maureen I'd been thinking of something else entirely when she'd revealed the sex of her baby.

"I've found it. A present for Maureen's baby." I pointed to the big pile of little rubber duckies. Ducks with Santa hats. Ducks on surfboards. Hawaiian ducks. Ducks wearing tuxes. They were darling, would fit in a carry-on, and the best part? Non-gender-specific.

"I remember she got Jack some little fish bath toys that squirted water. So this is perfect," I said, so darn excited, so darn proud that I had found a way out of the embarrassment of forgetting her baby's sex.

"Oh and look! Here is a little bathrobe." In yellow. "We're buying these."

"Are you sure you want to get her that?" Gabe asked.

"Yes. It doesn't matter if she's having a boy or a girl. These work no matter what. Plus, they're cute. I'm totally off the hook."

"I still think you should just ask Maureen."

Humph! What did he know? Maybe he wasn't the one for me? Maybe we *had* run our course? What if I did change direction? What if, instead of waking in my own Groundhog Day effect, I did something off-the-wall?

I considered Ferdie's advice against the five possible responses to conflict:

1. Solve the problem.
2. Change how you feel about it.
3. Accept it.
4. Stay miserable.
5. Make it worse.

Five and four were definitely out; I might have dab-
bled in misery here and there, but I certainly wasn't
committed to a life of suffering. To me, option three was
a choiceless choice; another version of mediocrity, like
Subarus in Colorado. That left me with option two: stay
and be happy with what we have. Or option one: Leave,
for something unknown on the horizon: maybe a baby,
maybe another loving life partner, but maybe not.

Was I willing to give up the love I had for a maybe?

Sometimes, I thought the answer might be yes.

Chapter 22

Birthing

Fresh starts, like birth, are the mint tea of life. I like mint tea. I also like the idea of birthing things: ideas, books, shopping sprees, a new home. I loved giving birth to my son. When I was pregnant, I felt special. Pregnancy was exciting. Everyone was happy with me and for me. A new hope was growing in my belly. I didn't know what to expect; the mystery endeared me to the process, like crafting a story where characters react in surprising ways.

I hadn't yet been able to answer Gabe's constant question of "Why did I want to have a baby?" I had, however, begun to notice that my urge to have a baby was stronger than ever when I felt otherwise worthless. I hadn't told Gabriel this. He might use this confession as ammunition in our ongoing pregnancy/baby debates. Nor had I told him that deep, deep, deep down, I suspected one of the reasons I wanted to have a baby was to excuse myself from publishing a novel.

Babies are the perfect out, after all. Don't have time or energy to be a published author? Of course not: have a baby! As a matter of fact, becoming a mother to a new-born was the be-all and end-all reason to not accomplish anything, ever (besides raising a human being, which is arguably, an enormous accomplishment). No one, and I mean no one was going to question why I would choose my child over being a novelist. Sure, some moms were superhuman and could accomplish all sorts of amazing stunts, all with their child dangling from their tit. I, though, wasn't one of those energetic multitaskers. For me, it was a choice between being the best mother I knew how to be, or something else. If I had a baby, I could hide behind an elegant mask. I could keep on nursing and pretending that not being a good enough writer didn't matter, 'cause hell, I'm a mother. Isn't that enough?

Besides, I'd dreamed of being an author for so long that becoming one, doing the work, seemed almost pathetic to want anymore. It seemed as if a timeline existed for dreams, and if a dreamer didn't achieve greatness or success within a "reasonable timeframe" the dreamer would be sent out to creative pasture.

Of course, I questioned my own timetable excuses, as I could always hear someone plugging Thomas Edison: "You know, he invented 786 light bulbs before he made the one that worked?" Yes, yes. Good for ol' Tommy. But I wasn't Thomas Fuckin' Edison. Such inspiration from others had little effect when my own gut felt like 500 gallons of water and electric wires connected to outlets with someone at the ready to flip the switch and burst my innards like fireworks. No matter what I did, I remained paralyzed with the kind of anxiety that led me to believe I was no good at the one thing I really wanted to do.

I didn't yet understand the lesson that talent was subjective. Worse still, I had not yet realized that the only reason for me to write was for pure joy. I didn't yet know that I could do art for art's sake. I thought I had to "be practical", "study business," and "make good money" as I'd heard over and over again since I was twelve.

Years later, I would recognize those runaway trains of inherited conversations. But back then, when Maureen was pregnant and I longed to give birth, I didn't know how to stop the assumed truths that I'd picked up from Mom, Dad, TV, embittered elementary school teachers, or even my own little five-year-old interpretations of adult-speak. The clichés ruled me. I fought against the unfairness of creating within the perceived starved, dry landscape of "ordinary, everyday American life." Then, I fought against my bad attitude toward the unfairness. I fought against lack of energy. I fought against time. I fought against responsibilities of work and motherhood. I fought against the proverbial hands around my neck.

No matter the fight, "I gotta get published" became a warrior cry that let me off the hook from ever writing. I continued the dialogue that looped me in the round-about of creating, and the biochemistry that reinforced my lethargy, anxiety, and depression. I didn't yet have a name for what I experienced. I only knew that I woke up fighting each day for happiness, self-expression, and the courage to tackle small tasks, like checking the P.O. Box. Some days, I gave a good fight; I took a walk despite not wanting to. Some days words were typed onto the page. Some days I even liked what I wrote. Some days, I just called Maureen.

Together, over the phone, wishing we could be face to face, she and I went through the list of usual pregnancy call-and-responses.

How have you been feeling; do you have morning sickness? Yes, some. I was really tired, but am better now. It's been pretty easy. I'm doing a lot of yoga.

Can you feel the baby kicking? Yes, it's so weird.

Is James excited? He's looking forward to being a dad.

Are you ready for this? I hope so. I never thought I would feel this way, but I'm in love with this child already.

Then as Maureen asked me, "Are you all right? You seem so vulnerable?" I instantly felt bored with myself and wondered if she felt that way too. Maybe Maureen would get awfully tired of picking me up over and over again, maybe even throw me away in the garbage, or to the dog, as a chew toy.

Still, I told her that sometimes I woke up crying. I told her how some days I didn't even have the energy to do a load of laundry. How Gabe cooked for me, and cleaned, and we watched a lot of movies. This talking to Maureen helped, so I told her more. I told her I couldn't count on myself. One minute I would be laughing, the next, beating my fist against a pillow. I told her I had to sleep a lot. Some days I didn't even want to wake up. I told her I felt angry. So angry. I loved Gabe. I hated that he didn't want to get married or have babies. I told her I wanted to have a baby. I told her I also thought it was crazy to want a baby. I had a child; he's wonderful, I told her. I think I should put all the baby-energy into mothering Jack. But, I told her, if I do, then I might suffocate him. I told her I'm writing some days and have ideas for a novel, but I wish I were writing more. I've been trying to shove it in between mothering and working and crying, I said. She told me again that she loved reading my blog and wanted more, please, more. I felt held: the warmth of a womb.

"I think I might be sick. Really sick," I said finally.

Over the years, I learned that the innate being-ness of humans is one of love and joy. I have felt that highest part of me many times, too many times to ignore. I have seen humans ripped to shreds by a tragedy and still break what little bread they have and laugh. I now know that when I'm gripped by irrational thoughts of "why bother" or "so-and-so won't like it" that those are valuable clues, meant to be cherished, appreciated, and followed to find the source.

At that time, I didn't know to follow the source. I didn't know what to do. I did the best I could, but I cried because I couldn't imagine going another ten years, let alone thirty or forty, without the taste of full authentic expression. For as much as I turned my back on self-expression, I also couldn't bear the thought of turning my back on self-expression. Each time I turned toward my truth, peeked out of the hole, I would scurry back in; a crab in the sand. I cried for fear that even with a friend like Maureen, I'd never find my way out.

"Have you tried sticky notes?" Maureen asked.

"Huh?"

"My life coach gave me this exercise. Write out what you want on sticky notes. Only one thing per sticky note. Then read it before you go to bed at night. And imagine what it feels like to have what you want." She paused. "You could try it."

I carried Maureen's sticky note idea with me to Pet Smart with Gabe on a routine errand. We stood, set in our ways, in the checkout line, watching the giddy girl behind the counter swipe the discount card for the thirty-pound bag of dog food.

"Three dollars off!" she exclaimed. The wrinkles in her forehead rippled upward, then straightened. She looked star-crazed. "What do you do for a living?" She only had eyes for Gabe.

"Uh, well. . . ." He stumbled, not sure if he ought to answer. Maybe we should call the cops.

"Are you a hockey player?" she asked, nodding her head, willing it to be so.

For that brief moment, I watched as the whole world landed in her eyes and she was certain she knew who he was, even if he wouldn't tell. A dream had walked through her ordinary line; it had to be.

And, in the moment her magical idea collided with my static world. I saw him through her eyes and wondered about the hockey player whose arm wrapped around mine.

"No. I'm afraid not," he said at last. "Like my son says, I just work at the computer all day and talk on the phone."

"Oh. You look like a hockey player." Then she turned and smiled at the next customer.

For me, the change in perspective was another hit of mint on my tongue. Did it really only take the simple alteration of one idea to reinterpret a truth? Could a simple sticky note—with a fresh idea spoken over and over again until I believed it—change everything?

As I look back on "baby wanting years" with distance, space, and some wisdom, I can see the only thing missing was a possibility. I'd gotten so caught up in the day-to-day that I forgot to invent. I no longer questioned the mantras, assumed truths, or even my own desires. Quite simply, I hadn't created a future that I wanted to live into.

Chapter 23

Fountain of Youth

Every life transition begins with a haircut. I never know how, when, or why they come about, but I woke up with a strong urge to cut my hair.

"So what do you want today?" Jessica, my hairdresser, escorted me to the barber chair. She pumped the foot lever, and the chair rose a few inches, lifting me with it: a middle-aged woman's amusement park ride. Jack lived for roller coasters; he wouldn't be very impressed.

"Just a trim. Maybe a couple inches. Same thing you did last time." I wanted fresh, not too daring. I wasn't looking for a cliff dive, just a small shift to tune my heart.

She led me to the beadboard room and shampooed me like a wet dog, all the while gabbing with another hairdresser shampooing another middle-aged woman like me. I couldn't hear what they were saying with the water spigot roaring around my ears like helicopter blades.

Jessica finally shut the water off. "There you go." I

sat up on cue as she wrapped a white towel around my head and pointed to the barber chair, where I plopped easily. I watched in the large wall mirror in front of me as she velcroed the cape over my shoulders.

"God, I hate my forehead." I didn't mean to say it out loud.

"There's nothing wrong with your forehead," she said and bopped across the room to get a fresh pair of scissors. I kept looking at myself in the mirror while she snipped away at my brown, graying hair.

"I'm getting older." I didn't like losing the feeling of having my whole life ahead of me, plenty of life left to make a writer of me.

"What makes you say that?"

"I don't know. Something's changed. Something's different. I look at my face and it doesn't look the same anymore. My skin isn't perky anymore. I've just been noticing it this last week. My mom always said this would happen. I never believed her."

"How old are you?" She grabbed a clump of hair on either side of my face, compared the lengths in the mirror, then let go and started cutting again.

"Thirty-six," I said on a big exhale.

"Really? You look so young for your age."

She was twenty-something. What did she know? *Snip, snip.* More hair landed on the floor.

Jessica rambled on. "My fountain of youth is denial and Botox. I've already started lying about my age."

"You're kidding?" I asked. She was so young; why would she lie?

Jessica tilted my head down to trim the back ends. "Don't move." *Snip. Snip.* "I'm serious; every couple of years, I take back another year," she continued her rationale. "That way it won't be so obvious as I get older. When I'm thirty-five, I'll have a thirty-year birthday party."

I stared at her in the mirror. I watched as she swished from one side of my head to the other, pulling tight strands of hair, chopping the ends, scissors mashing. She was quick, a product of youth. She said something else, but I couldn't hear.

"I said, it also works in reverse," she repeated herself. "I'll tell people I'm sixty when I'm only fifty, so they'll say, 'Wow, you look great for your age.'"

"That's quite a plan." I thought she was crazy.

"I think it's genius," she said. *Snip, snip. Snip, snip.*

"Yes, indeed." I wondered if I could pull off this kind of scheme. Would I even want to? "I think it's too late for me. So, what are you reading right now?" I always asked her this.

"*Life of Pi.* I read this book every summer. I have seasons of reading. Summers are fun and entertaining. Winters are for more intense reads."

Maybe it was not my season to write. Maybe I needed to wait until winter. Waiting seemed like the thing I did best: waiting until I graduated high school. Waiting until I graduated college. Waiting until I moved into a new house. Waiting until after Jack was born. Waiting until I got home from work. Waiting until I could leave my marriage. Waiting until Gabe and I were more comfortable with each other. Waiting until the dog was no longer a puppy. Waiting for the right time that never came.

Jessica talked like any self-respecting Southern hairdresser: continuously. "I'd love to be able to write, but I don't think I have any ideas. All I ever think about is hair." *Clip, snip, clip.* "I could write a book called *Clippers.*" She laughed.

"I can see it now. The next big Broadway musical."

"Like *Hairspray.*"

"Yes, exactly." I smiled too, feeling lighter with each strand she cut.

A woman poked her head in the back door just then and blurted out, "Jessica, sweetie, let Miss Bea know those vines outside are choking her air conditioning unit." The Southern drawl was thick with a hint of New Orleans proper.

"Sure thing, Miss Mary. Hey, how is your sweet boy doing?"

"Bless his soul, we're taking him up to Old Miss soon. It's going to be an empty nest. . . ."

I stopped listening. In the space of their dialogue, I got an idea for a scene in the novel and felt my own excitement build. I wished I had a piece of paper; I scanned the room to see what I could use instead and caught my eyes in the mirror. They looked brighter somehow.

When Miss Mary left, and Jessica turned her attention to me, I said, "If you want to write, just write. Don't worry about how it comes out. Just write."

"It's my fountain of youth," I added; I was done feeling like an old sticky note that kept falling off the fridge to the ground, warped from humidity and barely sticky. I was ready for my future.

I couldn't help but imagine the little girl in my novel and vines growing, tangling, choking the letters of the word b-o-y. As soon as I got to the car, hair primped, I wrote the beginning of a paragraph that wouldn't leave me alone:

She became steel. Johnny refused to feel even a cap full of crush. Instead, she imagined the letters that made up the word 'boy.' She saw the letters turn into vines and the tail of the "y" grew and grew until it choked the letter 'b' and covered the 'o' and left nothing but the tangle of thorny, viney weeds where just a moment ago stood an eleven-year-old. Nothing good would come of liking a boy.

I looked out the car window, wondering who would drive by. Someone you know is always driving by in a small town. They then tell someone else, who tells someone else, who then eventually tells the boss. My lunch hour was over.

I felt so happy that I felt guilty. I was afraid of getting caught, shoplifting minutes, writing in secret on the back of bank slips in a parked car. I was getting away with more than a long lunch break. I was getting away with joy. Purpose. Alignment. Was it wrong to feel so ecstatic? Was it wrong to roam with the word, to be let loose with my voice, when others continued on with forgotten dreams and shelved art? Would someone choke it out of me?

Even as I questioned myself, I understood I *needed* to roam with the word. Just like I needed natural sunlight, an unfixed schedule, a twist of lime. Just like I needed a bike with a basket in front to carry my daisies and fresh vegetables from the farmer's market. I needed a laptop to carry-on and a rubber band on my wrist for last minute ponytails. I absolutely needed to get my hair cut, to schedule an overdue appointment with the dermatologist (Granny would be proud). And I needed to make the time to write, no matter what.

In the back of the car, late for work, scribbling ideas, I felt this life of moles, zigzags, hairdressers, hands, doubts, and ballpoint pens weaving together to release the chokehold and carry me forward.

Chapter 24

Washing Machine

As I tucked Jack into bed, he read me a story he'd been writing at school about Mr. Edward who likes to eat and always wears a hat. When he finished, he turned to me.

"Mom, why don't you finish your novel and then you can publish it like that one author?" he asked, referring to Elizabeth Gilbert, whose book *Committed* rested on my nightstand.

"I would like to," I said.

"Well, I'm going to write a chapter a night. And when I'm done, do you think I can publish it?" he asked.

My heart went gooey like hot caramel. "Of course," I said, believing in him, but still unsure about my own publishing potential. What kept me wanting to hide when something brewed inside, something that wanted to be set free?

I watched him a moment, then leaned over and

kissed his forehead. "Psst. I think I want to visit the moon. Wanna go?"

"No way!" he said without a flicker. "I'm too scared. I'll stay with my dad when you go to the moon."

In Jack's fear, I instantly recognized my own. As his mother, I would have to show him how to be brave. I could only do that by modeling bravery myself.

Jack, without meaning to, had saved me over and over again. I was once scared to leave his father; it was wanting a brighter future for Jack that gave me the courage to leave. And now, I was scared to write; yet Jack showed me that I must, so that he too could learn how to follow his own heart and truth.

With all the bravery talk, a faint recognizable feeling gripped me. I turned off Jack's bedroom lights and found my way into my own room to snuggle under the comforter in safety while I waited for Gabe to finish brushing his teeth.

"I talked to Ferdie today. Guess what?" he asked as he walked into our bedroom and stepped into his pajama pants.

I yawned without looking up from the page. "What?"

"Ferdie and Josie are getting married."

The sheets fell to my lap; I sat straight up. "Getting married?" Ferdie said he would never get married again. "Really? Getting married?" I asked again. How could the jokester Ferdie have agreed to "I do" when my man was still holding onto his deflatable mattress?

"Yes, and they are trying for a baby," Gabe added.

Why, with all the happy words and hair I'd gotten out of my system, did I still care about making babies?

"Sweetie, what's wrong?" Gabe grabbed my hand, pulled me toward him. He wanted to hug me, comfort me. I wanted to fight. I wrangled free, terrified I'd go back to being breakable.

"Come on," he pleaded, almost forcing me to turn around.

"Tom, stop!" I didn't realize I'd yelled my ex-husband's name until Gabe walked out of the room, shrunken.

I don't know why I called out Tom's name except that it's the name I'd called out for so many years when I felt beaten, scared, angry, unloved, not enough. Maybe, calling out his name meant that Gabe wasn't the one I thought he was. Just like Tom hadn't been the one. Maybe Gabe didn't love me enough. Maybe I should say goodbye now.

"Yeah right." That now-familiar muse voice snarked. "There ain't no way that Tom and Gabe are alike. Think again, lady." He was right, of course. One man choked me, the other loved me. That I would respond in the same way to them both caught me off guard. As I ticked through the footage of my past, I found the phrase "not enough" in hidden alcoves of past relationships: in a high school crush with a dark renegade and his lusting hands, in a college love affair with Mr. Super Nice who killed with his forehand, in my first marriage with the bully, and now in the relaxed Euro-stride of the ever-loving Gabe. The men were the variables.

Before I could think it, the smart-ass muse in my head slapped me with iron truth: "It's you who is acting like the same woman."

I remembered telling my mother once when I was six years old that I wanted to win Wimbledon. I don't remember her exact response, but what my young, un-evolved brain heard her say was, "You'll never win Wimbledon." I was devastated to learn that I wouldn't win no matter what I did, and the haunting feeling that nothing I ever did would make any difference stayed with me. Therefore, I'd lived my life from the story that no matter how much I practiced tennis or writing or anything else for that matter, I would only get so far. The rest was unattainable, and I remained forever not good enough.

Not good enough for Adam, or, ahem, Michael (or whoever that was).

Not good enough for Gabe to marry me.

Not good enough for Gabe to want to have babies.

Not good enough to be a published author.

Not good enough for myself.

All at once, I felt proud of the insight and cramped by its ugliness. I didn't want to admit to a soul what I'd discovered, but I knew that if I didn't throw a wrench in the tango, I would repeat this dance card over and over and over.

If I could accept Gabe for who he is, everything he wanted and didn't want, then maybe I could accept me for who I was and everything I wanted and didn't want, even the teetering between opposing desires. For it was up to me to take those hands off my throat.

Whether it was my own self-loathing that enticed Tom's hands on my neck or his didn't much matter as I felt those hands ever at-the-ready to suffocate the life force they held.

In his grasp, I didn't write; I was afraid.

In his grasp, I didn't speak my mind; I was afraid.

I wish I hadn't given him so much power for so many years.

I wish I had seen that the moment he put his hands around my neck, the imprint had stayed for ten years, an invisible noose choking an already vanishing voice.

It wasn't until I saw the fear in Jack that I saw his father's hand still gripped me.

And not just Tom's hands, but all the metaphorical hands of those who came before to squelch out life, dreams, ideas, and will. Even those who meant well in their guidance and advice to "get good grades" and "be a good girl" became reminders not to tug too hard or the noose would tighten. They were the multitude of hands that led me to fear my life and the living of it. Tom's hands were simply the physical representation of all the moments before and after that felt like the choking of my self-expression.

It's hard to love when you are so damn angry.

It's hard to love when you are so damn afraid.

But I wanted love.

Yes, I was willing to send love to the man who put his hands on my throat.

Love doesn't mean surrender.

Love doesn't mean fall apart.

Love doesn't mean to let guards down and disappear behind someone else's veil.

Love doesn't mean I call once a week, or even once a year.

Love doesn't mean I have to accept bad behavior.

Love doesn't mean I have to stick around.

Love doesn't mean I have to serve Tom dinner, or invite him for Christmas.

I'd confused love with "being nice" for so many years. When Tom put his hands on my throat, I was glad because they showed me who he really was. At the same time, I was ashamed, because I felt I must have provoked him, wanting him to show his true colors. I wanted free of him, and I was glad he put his hands on my throat because then I would be justified in leaving him. I was ashamed because I wasn't brave enough to just leave. I wasn't brave enough to say no.

When he said, "You can't leave me. No one will understand why. I'm a good guy; I don't beat you," I believed him.

When he threatened to take my son away from me, I believed him.

When he told me I was a terrible person, I believed him.

I don't know why I believed those things.

He lied most of the time, I knew. But I choose to believe his lies because over time, it seemed plausible I indeed had become bad.

I did break all the Lincoln Logs in half when my mother told me to take good care of them.

I did cheat on my fourth-grade spelling test, and probably many others.

I did sleep with a married man.

When Tom put his hands on my neck, I thought I deserved it.

Truth is, I'd put my own hands around my neck, long before Tom put his there. He was just the vocalist for hidden lyrics. Sure, Tom carried out his threats, he lied, he bullied. He abused the mind of a young boy. He did all sorts of things that gave me cause to hate him. Hate his guts for all time. But I didn't hate him. I know why he made all those choices; he was scared too.

I couldn't save him from his fear; that was up to him. But I could recognize my own.

Now, I was the one who had her hands around my throat, making me afraid to post words on my blog, making me afraid to say what I mean. I told the lies, long before Tom told the lies. I believed the self-doubt long before I believed Tom. I was no longer bound by the delusions or required to align behind their truth. I could now say no.

When you lose your voice, you lose everything. In love, I could remove all the hands from around my neck. Love meant that I could accept my unique path, in my own way. In loving, I could move beyond fear and find my voice. Again and again.

I should thank Tom, really. That horrible, despicable, unlikable man. That funny, laughing, jovial man. I should thank him—for the anger, for the fear that he riled up until it burst out of me so strong that I had no choice but to release, sprout, and fly.

The next day, when I talked to Granny, I came to discover that when the hands were gone, I could breathe again, I could feel again, and I was no longer in a hurry.

"I had a surgery about five years ago. That might explain my craziness," Granny said, during the quick phone conversation. Granny had always been crazy in the best way.

"I know. I was worried about you," I said.

"I was worried about me too. I'm of the age to die, you know. I could go up there. Or maybe I'll go down. I'm not sure which. I don't have a reservation yet."

I laughed, loving my grandmother. Loving that I came from her cloth. Thinking that I would like to be her one day. Fabulously crazy.

But I didn't have a reservation yet either; there was time.

I had cracked the eggshell and found the yolk of a human who had lost belief in herself. I was an ordinary, extraordinary mole with a grandmother and a shredded alibi, expecting others to dish out the self-love and acceptance I didn't know how to provide to and for myself, from myself. Yet, when I began to spy on the "should I" or "shouldn't I" from the lens of self-worth, the answers became simple.

I wish I could say that all decisions from that moment on became easy, that I listened to my heart, heard the answer, and put my foot on the gas. Instead, I teeter-tottered still, forgetting, remembering. Forgetting, remembering.

But at that moment, I reveled in the glorious light

that there was nowhere I had to be, no success I had to achieve, other than the one I chose. I had no special purposes, except the ones I invented for myself. My life's meaning could not come from Gabe, or a publisher, or even a child.

Enough of being in the washing machine of marriages and babies!

Following Maureen's advice, I grabbed a blue Sharpie, along with a pile of sticky notes, and wrote the permissive words a friend of mine had typed on the neighbor girl's vintage typewriter: *It's okay to be a little crazy and to want to write*.

Chapter 25

Pregnant

Gabriel waited for me outside the security gate when I flew home from Maureen's baby shower.

"Welcome home, my darling." Gabe, always the excited puppy when we reunited after a day or a week apart, asked, "How was the baby shower?" and took me into a big bear hug.

"Sweet. Fun. Nice. The usual. Cake. Gifts. Women. Maureen has lovely friends."

"Did she like your yellow gifts?" he chuckled.

"She seemed to."

He grabbed my computer bag off my shoulder and slung it over his. "So? Do we know the sex?"

"Nope."

"Still?"

"There was no indication. Nothing predominately blue or pink."

"Strange." We walked hand in hand to the car.

"Do you know your best friend once told me I should break up with you if I wanted to have babies."

"Oh, great." His voice was playful, gentle, rolling his eyes in laughter as he took my hand in his and walked me to the car. I laughed too, no longer thinking about wanting and not wanting.

When Gabe and I got home, he took me to bed, kissing me, missing me, finding me, and I didn't think about babies. I was pregnant already, with stories, with love.

Epilogue

What It Took

To complete the first draft, it took being mad. Fighting for space. Fighting for my time. Taping pictures of all the characters to the living room wall.

Then it took taking the collages down when company came. Then taping them back up. Then moving them to the laundry wall, then the bedroom wall.

It took typing words (thousands of them) when I was irritated, distracted, clean, dirty, withdrawn, sick, hungry, cramping from my period, blue, and tired. It took typing words (thousands more) when I was excited, confident, preferring the company of the characters, and high from my month-long cleanse.

It took writing what I didn't know to write, writing what I did know to write, and loving every minute of it.

It took lying about what I was doing. And telling the truth about it. And knowing these words would haunt me forever if I didn't write them.

It took polite smiles to the woman at the coffee shop who wouldn't stop talking to me while I was typing.

It took telling the hands around my neck to "shoo," to "get, go on, scat." At times I felt the hands tightening; I wasn't sure they would ever completely go away. But they no longer had the power to strangle.

It took not being good enough, no matter how hard I tried. It took being willing to say, "The first draft of my novel is done" and that the result *is* good enough.

OMG, the first draft of my novel was done!

Even though my word count was less that I thought it would be.

Even though the neighbor character that dressed in houndstooth wouldn't identify himself. And the lake where the heroine lived didn't have a name.

It took three weekly calls with Ellie, a real person, not a character, to keep me sane.

It took saying "no" to some social engagements and "yes" to others.

It took a lot of girl time so the worries about my parents, money, or how I'm going to keep on living with Gabe didn't get in the way.

It took morning smoothies and sometimes hiding with my computer under the covers.

It took skipping yoga and adding it back in.

Sometimes it took vegetables, sometimes it took cookies.

It took wanting and wondering.

Then one morning, it took being willing to accept that, no, I didn't need to write another thousand words.

The first draft was done. The first draft was done. The first draft was done!

Because of it, I reaffirmed, I can count on myself.

Sometimes I am sidetracked, or sideswiped.

Sometimes (every morning!) despair and doubt get in, but I would always bounce back, always have.

And so it continued. . . .

The dog slept next to me, and I wrote.

Emails came, clients called. I wrote.

Holidays lingered, three chocolate truffles remained, and the man in the other room spoke of love and dates and maybe a walk together.

Still, I wrote.

I wrote for Maureen. Because Maureen fell in love with Johnny Rose; she wanted to know what would happen to the little girl.

And I wrote for me because writing brings me bliss. Because it's how I make sense of fever, grace, yearning, and the shocking joyride of everyday switchbacks.

Thank you, Lisa, for punching out on Ava's new typewriter the exact words I might have needed to know: *It's okay to be a little crazy and to want to write.*

It's okay to be a little crazy and to want.

Acknowledgments

A special thanks to the doulas who helped birth *The Elegant Out*:

Corinne, this book began as a gift to you and our friendship. Though it morphed into another story, you are the heartbeat without which this book, and (hello!) life as I know it, would not have survived.

Cameron, all the bold steps I've taken have been because of you. I love you more than you will ever be able to imagine until you have your own children. It is my great honor to witness your unique journey.

Wise Women (Annie Rose-Candace-Danya-Ellie-Kate-Lettecia-Martha-Sara-Shoshanna), A women's circle is a gift. You love me and see the best in me and believe in me, no matter how many years it takes me to come around.

Annie Rose, compadre in writing, editing, life creation, and cursing. Your turn.

Martha, matriarch of proofing. T-God for you. You see what my eyes, having scanned this manuscript a hundred times, no longer can.

The Write Club (Jonathon, Carrie, JoJo, Ryan): A brilliant crew! Remember the first draft? Yikes. Your insights, suggestions, and cut-to-the-chase feedback saved *The Elegant Out*.

Robin, if you hadn't strummed your guitar in the back of your SUV at that conference years ago . . . if I hadn't stopped to sing a song with you, stranger . . . if we hadn't clicked . . . if you hadn't turned writing coach . . . if I hadn't called you that day . . . if you hadn't believed when I didn't. . . .

Serena, the ultimate doula. You healed, nourished, ran errands and kept me sane with Clubhouse nights, Netflix binges, The Nerdist podcasts, and yummy Indian food.

Mom and Dad, the original birthers, teachers and material. You made me strong.

Granny, I've always wanted to be like you. (Post-completion, Granny's reservation came. For sure, she went up.)

Monkey Muse, I'm listening. . . .

Ben, more than yesterday, less than tomorrow.

The extraordinary team at She Writes Press: You polished and made this book beautiful and took it over the finish line, supporting me every step of the way. More importantly, you advocate for and support authors' voices. Amen!

For all of you dear friends and readers who lit the fire under my ass with your constant question: when you gonna finish your book? Do it again, please.

And, dare with me!

xoxo,

Elizabeth

About the Author

Photo credit: Ann Dinwiddie Madden

Praised as a "word colorist" with a distinct lyrical style and unflinching strokes, Elizabeth Bartasius is a writer and editor of transformative stories that inspire and engage. *The Elegant Out*, her debut novel, placed as a finalist in the 2017 Faulkner–Wisdom Competition. She enjoys European cafes, tropical climates, and list-making. She currently lives in the US Virgin Islands with her husband and a rogue iguana. Visit her and read more at www.elizabeth-bartasius.com.

SELECTED TITLES FROM
SHE WRITES PRESS

She Writes Press is an independent publishing company founded to serve women writers everywhere.
Visit us at www.shewritespress.com.

The Geometry of Love by Jessica Levine. $16.95, 978-1-938314-62-9. Torn between her need for stability and her desire for independence, an aspiring poet grapples with questions of artistic inspiration, erotic love, and infidelity.

A Drop In The Ocean: A Novel by Jenni Ogden. $16.95, 978-1-63152-026-6. When middle-aged Anna Fergusson's research lab is abruptly closed, she flees Boston to an island on Australia's Great Barrier Reef—where, amongst the seabirds, nesting turtles, and eccentric islanders, she finds a family and learns some bittersweet lessons about love.

Play for Me by Céline Keating. $16.95, 978-1-63152-972-6. Middle-aged Lily impulsively joins a touring folk-rock band, leaving her job and marriage behind in an attempt to find a second chance at life, passion, and art.

Shelter Us by Laura Diamond. $16.95, 978-1-63152-970-2. Lawyer-turned-stay-at-home-mom Sarah Shaw is still struggling to find a steady happiness after the death of her infant daughter when she meets a young homeless mother and toddler she can't get out of her mind—and becomes determined to rescue them.

Anchor Out by Barbara Sapienza. $16.95, 978-1631521652. Quirky Frances Pia was a feminist Catholic nun, artist, and beloved sister and mother until she fell from grace—but now, done nursing her aching mood swings offshore in a thirty-foot sailboat, she is ready to paint her way toward forgiveness.

Magic Flute by Patricia Minger. $16.95, 978-1-63152-093-8. When a car accident puts an end to ambitious flutist Liz Morgan's dreams, she returns to her childhood hometown in Wales in an effort to reinvent her path.